And The Time Came

Mason Davis

Published and Edited by Opportune Independent Publishing Company

Printed in the United States of America

Books may be purchased in large quantity and/or special sales by contacting Littlerocmanagement@gmail.com or visiting www. masondavisworks.com.

PREFACE

"If growing up is painful for the Southern Black girl, being aware of her displacement is the rust on the razor that threatens the throat. It is an unnecessary insult."

— Dr. Maya Angelou,
I Know Why the Caged Bird Sings

TABLE OF
CONTENTS

CHAPTER ONE

———◦———

E ricka! Chanel! Monique! It's time to get up!"

Chanel detested awaking to that annoying wakeup call every "morning. The sound of their mother's voice jolted her and her sisters out of their sleep every morning. Next came the hustle and bustle of the girls getting ready for school, with the usual traffic jam just to get into the bathroom to brush their teeth and wash their faces. But not today–today was different. It's the last day at their current school. However, it wasn't the end of the school year, but it was to be the end of Chanel's boring life in Jacksonville, Texas. A new life was awaiting. They were moving to Bakersfield, California.

The family had been busy for weeks packing their belongings and having garage sales to earn extra cash, while lightening their load for the long upcoming trip. California was going to be a welcomed change. Jacksonville was not just small, but it was as country as small towns come. Their town wasn't dubbed a nickname as catchy or as cool as the "City of Angels." Instead, it was nicknamed the "Tomato Capital of the World," and had a population of less than 15,000. What pre-adolescent girl wouldn't be bored out of her mind in a town like that? Chanel had been looking forward to this move for a long time. It was perfect–for the first time in her life, she believed she had a real chance at doing something spectacular.

Chanel hurried to get dressed, not just in excitement, but also because they were running a little late. She went downstairs, put together some breakfast, and sat down to eat while she waited for the others to get ready. As she sat, she couldn't help but think of Joe—Chanel and her younger sister's, Monique, biological father. Ericka considered him her daddy too, probably because he and their mother met so early in her life.

A few years before their father and mother separated, she raised them alone. As disappointing as it sounds, it probably was best that her parents were no longer together. Her father was much older than her mom, by at least ten years. Plus, he had too many issues to name. He wasn't even a part of their lives when they were living together.

The marriage didn't last long. In fact, they didn't even get married until Chanel was nearly four, and their relationship was rocky from the start. The two met at a house party a year before Chanel came along.

"Kathy, you should come with me to Maxine's birthday party tonight" Juanita, *their mother's sister, suggested. Maxine was Juanita's best friend since the first grade.* "Remember that bad dude from California Max and I met at KFC the other day? Max invited him. So he might be there." *It was the seventies, so it was cool to talk like that.*
Kathy rolled her eyes and said, "Nah Juanita, I'm not interested."

"Oh come on girl. It's just one night out!" Juanita begged. "You should unwind a little! We both need a break from our kids."

She looked at Juanita and thought for a moment. "Alright, I'll go," Kathy said. You know Nannie is not going to want to watch the kids again...

Kathy knew why. Juanita's estranged husband had been in prison for over a year now, and would likely be there for the next ten, but she was still devoted to him. Kathy and her nine-month-old baby girl Ericka, had moved in with Juanita and her little boy, just weeks after her husband was locked up. So, the kids came as a package from that point.

At first, their mother gave them grief about dropping off their babies so late and unexpectedly, but always would eventually give in. Like this particular night.

After the kids were with grandma, it was time to party. The sisters arrived late, but the house party was still full well after midnight. Kathy was less than enthused already because it was the middle of March and unusually cold outside.

"Hey, Max!" Juanita tried to shout above the chatter of guests and music. The soulful "Darlin, Darlin Baby" by the O'Jays was blaring in the background.

"Heeeeey, where have y'all been?" Max replied.

"I had the hardest time deciding what threads to put on," Juanita said. She twirled around once and held out her arms. "How do I look?" Juanita, the aspiring beautician, had a real talent with cosmetics, but unfortunately, her fashion sense wasn't so inspiring. The green and orange bell bottom romper left everyone with questions that night.

But as a good friend, Maxine assured her and said, "Out of sight!"

"Hey, is that guy, Joe, here yet?" Juanita asked. "I want Kathy to meet him."

"Not sure," Max yelled. "He was earlier, but I don't see him now." The room was so jammed packed; they would have been hard-pressed to get a peek of the floor.

"Well, I sure hope he's still here," Kathy complained. "He's the only reason I showed up. I could be home watching Johnny Carson." Before those words could completely escape Kathy's ruby red lips, her eyes were drawn to a guy standing near the record player as if he were the designated deejay.

"Please tell me that's him," she muttered.

"Oh yeah, that's him. Joseph James Hamilton. Fine, ain't he?" Maxine answered.

"Out of sight," Kathy mumbled. She wondered to herself whether he'd come to the party alone, though she really didn't care. She had laid eyes on the man of her dreams and wasn't leaving that party without meeting him.

Joe was tall and slim, with a 3-inch afro. He had hazel eyes with matching caramel skin and a smile as dazzling as Nat King Cole's; definitely easy on the eyes. He was wearing a burgundy butterfly collar shirt with a pair of light blue polyester cuffed bell bottoms, over a pair of cowboy boots. Simply put... Joe was gorgeous, and he was effortlessly charming every single woman in the room. It's no wonder he captured Kathy's attention that night.

With all the confidence she could muster up, Kathy made her way to the deejay table and posted herself within arms reach of the grooviest man in the room. She watched intently as Joe sipped on a beer, trying to come up with the right thing to say to him.

"Your name's Joe, huh?" It was all she could come up with at the time.

"Say what?" he questioned. Joe could barely hear Kathy's soft voice over the music. By now, the sounds of Marvin Gaye's "Got To Give It Up," was sweeping through the steamy room.

"I couldn't hear you." He explained.

"I said, your name's Joe. Joe Hamilton, right?" Kathy repeated nervously, a little louder this time.

Why couldn't the young woman just leave it at that? Making his acquaintance would have been sufficient had she known the pain and heartache the sleek stranger would eventually bring to her life. There was a mystery about this guy. Why was such a beautiful man available anyway? Answering this question before continuing their conversation would have served Kathy in the best way, but Kathy was no different than a lot of woman. She needed to know more.

Joe, instantly attracted to the petite, busty younger woman, smiled back and said, "That's right. And who are you?"

"Katherine Banks, but everyone calls me Kathy." Their age dif-ference was the least of her concern, and clearly Joe wasn't worried about it.

That night, Kathy learned that 30-year-old Joe was divorced and had two children already; one from his marriage and the other from another previous relationship. He was very intelligent, a college graduate, and made good money working full-time for a railroad company. So he traveled a lot, which was more than Kathy could say for herself. She had never been more than 50 miles away from home in her life. Out of slight embarrassment, she didn't tell him about Ericka right away. How could she tell a stranger that she got pregnant by her teenage boyfriend while still in high school? Joe also withheld some important information—the fact he had a drinking problem. After some time of being indulged in comfortable conversation, Joe was still very much so intrigued. So, Kathy decided to tell him about her nine-month-old baby at home, she was sure she'd won the top prize because he barely flinched at the news. They talked for hours; long after the music stopped and Maxine's other guests started to leave.

"So, when do you think I can see you again?" asked Joe.

"I don't know. When can you make time for me?" Kathy coyly replied.

"Oh, I can always find time for the things I like. Why don't you give me your phone number and we can set something up?"

"You have Max's number, right? Why don't you just use that number to get a message to me?" Kathy said.

"Now why would I do that?" The sexy man was somewhat bewildered. "What is it? Your father won't allow you to have calls from men at home?" Joe hinted with a slight smirk.

"My father? I'm a grown woman. I don't need my daddy's permission for anything." She said it full of confidence, but deep

down inside Kathy was scared to death to even think of what her parents would say about her getting involved with a 30-year-old man. They would not be pleased, but she wasn't going to let Joe know that, at least not right now.

"It's just that I live with my sister right now," she explained, "And we don't have a phone." Kathy was a little embarrassed by this also, but it was better than seeming like a little girl who couldn't have boys calling the phone.

"Oh, okay. I understand," Joe said smiling. "I'll ring Maxine tomorrow to try and reach you," Joe agreed.

Kathy left the party that night on cloud nine. She had no idea the number of demons plaguing Joe's life that she would eventually fall victim to. They would go on to spending much quality time together. As he impressed her with his charm, she kept him intrigued with hers. In the following months, Kathy learned a lot about her prince charming. Things like Joe and his little sister nearly becoming orphans; they never had a chance to get to know their birth parents well.

Their young mother died of a postpartum hemorrhage hours after giving birth to Joe's sister. He was only four years old at the time. When their father abandoned them, they were shuffled around from one relative to the next. Eventually, the children went to live in Fresno, CA, with their great uncle and aunt. Fortunately, Joe and his sister were loved and raised with the best of everything. The remainder of their childhood was like a fairytale. Joe was gifted and popular in school— a true ladies man. But, he always struggled with the feelings of abandonment that his natural father left him with. He used his appeal to his advantage and left a lot of women hurt in the process. Joe became the love them and leave *them type, but never realized the one who left him and his sister years before, was the same man he was destined to become.*

Kathy knew Joe was divorced, but he didn't tell her that his two children were born in the same year to two different women. She needed to get answers from her new love interest, sooner rather than later.

A month after they had met, Joe, Kathy and her baby were out for lunch. "Maxine told me that your son and daughter are the same age, but they aren't twins. Is that true?" Kathy folded her arms as she looked at Joe from across the table with a slight shake of head back and forth.

A defensive Joe answered, "Well since you know everything, why don't you tell me?"

"I'm giving you the opportunity to tell me the truth," she fired back.

"Yeah. It's true. Is that a problem?" Joe questioned arrogantly.

"I really wish you had told me yourself. They're your children and you shouldn't be ashamed of them." Kathy was trying to sound mature.

"I'm not ashamed of my kids," he answered.

"Well, why didn't you tell me then?" she questioned.

"Because their mothers are not your concern."

Kathy, frustrated, let out a deep breath. "Well is there anything else I should be concerned about?" She wanted to make sure her family didn't have any more ammunition to help discourage this new relationship.

Joe leaned back in his chair, looked the young woman directly in her eyes and lied through his teeth as if he had nothing else to hide. Joe knew there was a possibility he was also the father of another woman's child. The woman, was six months pregnant, and Kathy knew her very well. She and Janice went to high school together, and she was the sister of Kathy's ex-boyfriend, Ericka's father.

Joe kept quiet about that secret and so many others.

He thought he was happy with Kathy, he had finally found someone to help fill that space he'd been carrying around for all of these years. He took her and Ericka to meet his family in California and they loved them. Kathy's parents weren't so accepting of him. They didn't trust Joe and really didn't like the age difference between the two.

"He's trouble. I can feel it in my bones," Her mother would say.

Kathy's mother, Nannie, had always been the discerning type— with five daughters, she needed to be. "He needs to find a woman his own age," Nannie insisted. "You'll be pregnant again before you know it."

Not to her surprise, Nannie was right. Kathy did get pregnant, and was expected to deliver not long after Ericka's second birthday. Chanel was born in the summer, and Joe denied he was her father from the moment Kathy announced she was expecting. So her birth certainly didn't change anything. The prince charming she'd come to know had morphed into a frog and hopped away. He was nowhere to be found when the baby arrived. In fact, he didn't see his new baby girl until she was nearly 4 months old.

Joe would bounce in and out of Kathy and her girls' lives for the next couple of years. As a young mother, Kathy struggled to care for her children. If it weren't for her parents and sister, she wouldn't have made it. They took care of the children when she was working, and even when Kathy got pregnant with Monique. One of the times when Joe was present, he managed to get her pregnant again. This time he believed he was the father right away, but it wasn't until Chanel and Ericka's baby sister was born did Joe accepted Chanel as his child too.

Monique was born months premature, which caused some challenges for her, like physical disabilities. Maybe the guilt of having a disabled child persuaded him to make a commitment to his not so new family or maybe it was just maturity. Nevertheless, Joe asked Kathy to marry him. She was thrilled, but her parents were not… rightfully so.

"Are you sure this is what you want to do?" Kathy's father tried to reason.

"Yes, daddy," Kathy answered. "I'm sure."

"Well, she's got three children now. There's nothing else for her to do except marry him," Nannie butted in.

"She doesn't need to marry him just because she has children, Nannie. She has to make the right decision and I know this isn't it," Kathy's father said adamantly.

"It's too late to think about what's right and what's not. She created

this situation for herself and now she has to live with it." It pained Nannie to say it because she was not a fan of Joe, but she knew life would be difficult for her grandchildren not having a father.

"Well, if it's the right decision or the wrong decision, it's mine to make," Kathy interrupted.

They all left it at that. A few months went by in order for things to calm down and for Kathy to lose a little baby weight.

The wedding was in her parent's backyard. Everyone was there— all of her sisters, brother, and cousins. Even Joe's sister and adoptive parents attended. Juanita was her matron of honor. The wedding was simple, yet an event to see. During the reception, a drunken Joe was loudly singing along with the music and dancing with every single woman, smiling that charming smile Kathy fell in love with that very first night at Max's apartment. She couldn't help but think, Now, I will have the life I've always wanted, and the one my girls deserve.

As great as she thought it would be, Joe didn't do Kathy any favors by marrying her. No one in the family spoke about him or even thought about the Joe they had come to know. The verbal abuse began when Kathy was pregnant with Chanel. The first time he hit her was the night after Chanel's first birthday party. That's when Kathy found out that he was in fact the father of her high school classmate's (and first daughter's aunt) little boy. She invited Janice and the child over to the party to be with Ericka. After all, Janice was Ericka's aunt and she hadn't seen her niece very much since she moved to out of town just before having her own baby.

Joe and Janice both kept quiet when they saw each other at the party; Neither said a word to the other. Janice however, decided to give Kathy a call the following day to fill her in. Kathy was in shock. She was so humiliated that Joe had managed to keep up appearances that long without coming clean about yet another child. She confronted him when he came home after work that night.

"Please tell me it's not true, Joe," she pleaded.

"I have no way of knowing for certain that he's mine," he insisted.

"I don't care if you don't believe he's your son, Joe. Is it possible?" Kathy asked with tears in her eyes.

"Well…" he hesitated. "I guess it's possible, but I don't know for sure."

"How could you make me look like a fool?" Kathy yelled.

Joe yelled back, "I told you I don't know for sure. Now stop pestering me about it!" he demanded as he slapped Kathy in her face.

Kathy's left cheek tingled and she could taste the bitterness of her own blood in her mouth. She didn't question Joe again about the child after that.

Kathy was even more afraid of Joe and the violence continued to escalate. Sadly, the young man didn't discriminate when it came to allowing the kids to witness it on nearly every occasion. Late one night, when the older girls were six and eight, they were awakened by the sound of bumps and thumps against the walls, followed by the piercing screams of their mother. Chanel and Ericka crawled out of bed, crouched down on their tiny hands and knees to peek through the space between the bottom of their bedroom door and the floor. They watched as Joe dragged Kathy by her hair down the hallway, kicking and screaming passionately, from their master bedroom and into the living room. The view from the space was their usual ring side seat. Next, there was the crash of glass shattering and the rumble of the floor felt like an earthquake.

The glass dining table was about five and a half feet long. It had been shattered so many times during her parents' brawls, even the six-year-old knew it was foolish to keep replacing it. Joe's drinking always set him off. As Chanel grew older, the only concrete memories of her father she held on to were those of him beating their mom.

Chanel lived in constant fear that she would come home from school and Kathy would be beaten, or worse, dead. Joe was so predictable that the girls anticipated a fight would happen any time they came home with Kathy after dark. It was as if their grown mother had a "streetlight" curfew like all of the children in the neighborhood.

One night Kathy and her girls had been visiting her sister, Juanita. When they jumped into the car to drive home, Chanel felt a knot growing in her belly as tight as one of those double fisherman's knots rock climbers use to secure their ropes. To escape the pain, she stared out of the backseat car window at the dark sky.

As they drove she asked, "Mama, will we be home soon?"
That was the six year old's way of urging their mother to put a little more muscle behind the gas pedal. Still, that shiny silver 1985 Camaro couldn't pick up enough speed for her. Chanel didn't want to watch Kathy get beaten up again, but they all would many more times.

When they walked into the house, the lights were off, but Chanel knew Joe was home because his black pick-up truck was parked out front. When Kathy turned on the light switch, they saw Joe sitting in a chair from the kitchen table. He had positioned himself directly in the path of the front door, so he would be the first thing Kathy saw when she walked in. By now, the girls knew the routine; Ericka quickly grabbed Monique from Kathy's arms and the girls scrambled out of the line of fire.

It was impossible for the girls to silence the deafening cries of their mother as she tried to fend off such a strong man. The children stood in the hallway watching wide-eyed as if it was their first time seeing this horror play out, with their hands covering their ears. As terrifying as it was, they wanted to know their mother was still holding on to dear life. After a stint of crying, Joe ordered them to go into their bedroom. Monique could sleep through anything, she was just a toddler and was still asleep from the car ride back home.

Kathy tried to plead her case. "Stop it, Joe!" she shouted. "We were at Juanita's. I swear."

From their room, Chanel could imagine Kathy kicking and scratching Joe, trying to fight back, but she was no match for him. The little girl crawled under the bed in an effort to take cover. With her hands over her ears, she curled up into a fetal position and closed her eyes as tightly as she could. She prayed that a neighbor or someone would hear the commotion and come save them all, especially her mom. But of course, no one came.

The next sound the little girl heard was, "Nel!, come out from under there." The family had nicknamed her "Nel" from birth. Chanel could feel someone tugging on her hand. She could see the sun piercing through the dingy white curtains in their bedroom from under the bed. She had fallen asleep under the bed again and her mother was there to pull her out.

"I've been calling your name for ten minutes now," Kathy bellowed. "It's time to eat breakfast."

Chanel and her big sister darted to the kitchen to eat their usual breakfast of piping hot oatmeal with toast.
"Hurry up and eat your food or you will be late for school," Kathy insisted.

It was the first day, and the girls were super excited. They would be a part of the very first students to attend the newly constructed facility. The opening was going to be broadcast on the local news and all the kids in their neighborhood felt like celebrities.

Chanel and Erika swallowed most of their breakfast without chewing, and scampered to their room to get dressed. Joe had left for work on the railroad before daylight and, as usual, he left $1 in quarters on the girls' dresser; 50 cents for Ericka, and 50 cents for Chanel to buy lunch.

Chanel sat at the kitchen table remembering how chaotic life when her father was around. She was looking forward to her new life in California and new school. She hoped her teacher would be nice and that she would make friends on the first day. Even though she was mostly shy and didn't like to speak much, Chanel was a friendly girl and felt good when someone noticed. Ten minutes had passed before she was snatched back into reality and remembered it was her turn to get her hair combed. Kathy yanked on her soft brown tresses as she sat up straight in the chair, and she was lost again. Her mother's yanking on her tender scalp barely hurt at all as she easily zoned out without a care in the world.

Good memories with her father, like the ones of the first day of first grade were few and far between for her and her sisters. Kathy and Joe parenting peacefully was something the young children had rarely seen. Now that the girls were older, Chanel in her 'tweens, and Ericka just getting started as a teenager, other things filled their thoughts. The big move to the west coast would be a welcomed new beginning for their small family-a fresh start. Everyone else may be having second thoughts, but Chanel was excited to be moving.

CHAPTER TWO

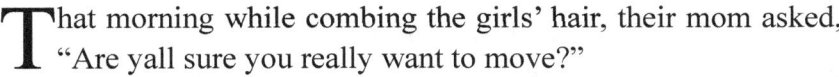

That morning while combing the girls' hair, their mom asked, "Are yall sure you really want to move?"

Chanel answered, "Yes" without hesitation, but not her sisters. Ericka was only 13, and by now, she was very much into her friends, so her mind was fixed on finishing junior high with her friends and Monique was too young to make such a decision.

"It's not too late if y'all want to stay," Kathy said.

"But Mama, what about our new house? It's really special. You said so yourself," Chanel reminded her.

"And the beaches - who wouldn't want to wake up to the smell of crisp ocean air?" Chanel was such the salesman.

"I know, I know," Kathy hushed her. "I haven't changed my mind. I'm just making sure you guys are okay with it."

Chanel didn't know what caused their mother to suddenly have second thoughts. A lot of planning had gone into this transition and she feared it would all be a waste.

Kathy had sold or given away nearly everything they owned. She wanted them to be completely free from the past and have a new beginning, free from all the bad memories. The house on Castle Road was the place they moved into after Kathy and Joe separated. It was a tacky house inside and out. It was black brick, with canary yellow shutters on the windows and siding. There was a hideous water well out front to match. It sat atop a hill in the yard and had likely not been operable since the 1930s, when the house was built. Every room inside the house had different color walls. There was the baby blue family room, a green and yellow kitchen with orange laminate floors, and peach wallpaper in the bathroom. The house was in Western Hills, historically a semi-affluent community, but it was definitely not in jeopardy of winning any Better Homes & Gardens prizes - not even as an honorable mention.

Nonetheless, the old house was a dream come true for Kathy. With the help of the government, she was finally able to give her kids a front and back yard to play in - something Joe never gave her and the children

Kathy reconsidering the move worried Chanel enormously. She didn't want to spend her life wondering how things would've been had the move not taken place. Would she have made the same life choices or different ones? Did the move really even matter at all?

Not long after all the questioning and wondering, the family did in fact move to California. The divorce was final, which signified the end of much more than the end of a marriage. This was the final chapter to a lot of hurt, pain and horrific memories. Things between Chanel and her father, however, were over much sooner. The man she knew as her mother's abuser became an object of resentment and a source of low self-esteem for her. Like a lot of young children of divorce, Chanel struggled to understand how her dad could leave and not look back for his children. This wasn't the first time for him, though. He had a reputation for leaving his kids. Chanel, in particular, would spend the next ten years of her life trying to comprehend why she seemingly wasn't loved enough, or enough to love.

The last time she laid eyes on their father was in court. Kathy had brought her along for one of their child support hearings. After the proceeding, Joe walked over and accused Kathy of being greedy and trying to take all of his money so he would be left in the poor house. He wanted the single mom to know he would never let that happen. He proved himself to be more and more selfish. Chanel didn't even believe Joe noticed she was there.

Their first sight of the California coastline was like a photograph.

"Mama, this is the prettiest place on earth," Ericka said.

Every window in the car was down as they all took in the warm ocean breeze. It was the middle of October, but it felt like spring. Juanita and her new boyfriend were following close behind in the U-Haul truck. An hour later, everyone came to a rest in front of a ranch-style blue and white stucco home.

The girls bailed out of the car and rushed for the front door of their new home.

"I know where my room is," Ericka shouted.

"Well, this is it!" Kathy looked back at Juanita and Greg. "I just hope I made the right decision."

"Girl, you can always come back home," Juanita assured her.

"Give it a fair shot, though. You just might fall in love with this place." I already have, she replied.

Chanel hoped they would make it there too, because she didn't want to go back to Texas. She thought it was best to be as far away from her father as possible, for Kathy's sake. Plus, since the split, Joe hadn't even called to check on the well-being of any of the girls.

Besides, he had many other kids he needed to worry about too. Everyone knew about Joe Jr. his son with his first wife, but Kathy kept the daughter he had outside of his first marriage a secret. Chanel and her sisters became somewhat close with Raymond Ericka's cousin and Joe's second son. He was the child Joe punished Kathy for when she inquired about him years earlier. Even though she was cautioned to never ask about the kid again, Kathy tried her luck by allowing her girls to spend time with him almost every weekend when they were young, even though Joe never approved.

Back when Kathy and Joe were still together, she would take the kids to Ericka's grandparents' house on her father's side sometimes for a visit. Most of Ericka's family would be there - including her first cousin, Raymond. Chanel remembered him as being tall and lanky, with the most beautiful pearly white teeth. Although they didn't see each other much, they were alike. He was pretty quiet too. In a very soap opera-like fashion, Joe knew he didn't need further proof that the boy was his, but he would never claim him as his son. Even as kids the girls knew better. It was all in the eyes. Raymond had the same dreamy hazel eyes his father had. Since Joe wasn't the most forthcoming about his kids, he didn't have a model relationship with any of them.

Chanel didn't miss her dad's physical presence, but she grew to despise how hard his financial absence was on their mother. Before they separated for good, Kathy was battling a setback of her own. As if raising three children as a single parent wasn't difficult enough, Kathy had lost her ability to work full time when she was injured in a serious car crash.

Once Ericka and Chanel were visiting Kathy's only brother, Jim in New Orleans for summer break. Uncle Jim and his wife, had their first child that summer, and the sisters were thrilled to be a part of decorating the nursery in baby pink. They even knitted a soft bunny shaped pillow for their new cousin. When the baby girl was one month old, Kathy came back with Monique to drive the big girls home to Texas. Minutes before they left the next day, everyone fought over who would hold the new baby in the farewell pictures.

"You held her already, Ericka," Chanel protested. *"It's my turn now."*

"Watch her head." Ann said as she planted the tiny infant into Chanel's skinny little arms.

"I'm going to miss you, little one." Chanel whispered in her ear. She kissed her cheek as Ann reclaimed her from the original tussle. Kathy and her girls jumped into her Camaro and hit the road. She loved that car, and she especially loved driving it on the highway. She nicknamed it Silver Bullet. It was actually birthday gift to her from Joe.
Louisiana summers were always Sub-Saharan hot, but the heat that day was especially oppressive. That's probably why the girls were asleep within an hour of starting the journey home. They were in such a deep sleep that all of the girls slept through the impact of their mother colliding head-on with another vehicle. The only

thing Chanel remembered before being pulled out of the wrecked vehicle by a middle aged white woman, was the finger-licking good drumstick and biscuit she was eating. Kathy had stopped at Kentucky Fried Chicken along the road for lunch. Fearing the youngster had a concussion, the paramedics labored snapping their fingers at her and shaking Chanel to keep awake after the wreck.

The emergency room was chaotic. Each member of the family was treated in different rooms, separated by those hospital curtains that looked like bed sheets. Chanel heard her sisters crying in all the commotion, and a delusional Kathy demanded the nursing staff to get her a cup of coffee to drink. Luckily, the girls sustained non-life threatening injuries; Ericka a dislocated jaw, Monique a broken leg, and besides the concussion, Chanel suffered cuts to her legs, knees, and hands from the shattered glass. She went into a panic when the doctors attempted to remove the glass from her skin.

"No, no, no. Mommy, no!" she shouted.

"Sweetheart we have to get the glass out of your hands," the nurse insisted. "It's not good for you."

Crying uncontrollably, Chanel repeated, "No, noooo."

Snatching her arms away and nearly falling from the table, Chanel resisted the treatment heavily. The staff resorted to wrapping her tiny hands behind her back to force her extremities into the solution that would help draw the glass fragments out. There were more tears and more screams than before. It was over in a matter of minutes. However, their mother wasn't so fortunate.

Kathy was hospitalized in Louisiana for over a month. Both her ankles had been crushed to pieces, and she was confined to a wheelchair for months before she would walk again. Kathy had driven less than 80 miles out of town before the crash, so Uncle Jim was contacted initially by the hospital. Within a couple of hours, he and Ann were there to be with the family.

Chanel's 7th birthday party was in Kathy's hospital room. Jim's wife was sweet enough to buy an ice cream cake with a big number 7 wax candle on it to celebrate. Ironically, it would be the only birthday cake Chanel remembered. It was an especially memorable time because later Uncle Jim registered Ericka and Chanel in school in New Orleans for a few weeks. He didn't want the girls to fall behind in school since they couldn't go back to school in Jacksonville until Kathy was released from the hospital.

When Kathy was finally released, their father came to pick them up with a customized van he'd rented. He brought his friend Gary along to help because he wasn't use to handling or transporting a disabled person. Poor Kathy was in so much pain - and that tumble off of the seat she'd taken in the back of the van while Joe was driving, only made the pain more unbearable.

"Dammit, Joe!" she yelled.

"What the hell?" Joe shouted as he slowed the van down.

"Daddy, she fell off of the seat," Ericka reported back.

Chanel saw the tears and realized her mother had never felt pain like that before; not even after one of her worst rounds at the hands of their dad. He pulled the van off the highway so that he and Gary could get her back in a comfortable position. Kathy was trembling with pain. Even the girls knew their mom's recovery would be a long one. Her doctors didn't expect her to ever walk again. If Kathy couldn't walk, she couldn't work, and not working was taking its toll, especially on Joe.

Kathy was working for a phone company before the accident, but she was laid off when she couldn't come back to work soon enough. Physically, it was impossible for her to work as she had done before. With Kathy down and Joe being the only bread winner, eventually the children became aware of the family's dependence on government assistance to fill in the gaps. While Kathy tried to regain her ability to walk, and their father stayed out drinking with his buddies, Ericka and Chanel took on the responsibility of taking care of the household. Not only were the nine and seven-year-old children nursing their mother back to health by emptying bedpans and redressing wounds, but they were also doing the grocery shopping, cooking, and cleaning. Of course, they would have preferred playing outside like the other kid in the neighborhood

Every morning before school, Kathy sent one of the older girls across the street to the 7-Eleven to buy her a Coca Cola and a honey bun. On one extra sunny morning, it was Chanel's turn.

"Okay Chanel, I want you to be sure to bring my change back. Remember, you forgot it last time?" Kathy reminded her. "Be careful and put on your sweater."

"Yes, ma'am," Chanel replied as she headed out of the front door. She hated that funky gray sweater! It was a hand-me-down from her cousin. The most hideous thing you could imagine; It had white pom poms lined around the collar with some of the strings pulled away from the pattern. Kathy always insisted on humiliating Chanel by forcing her to wear it, but it was a chilly morning, and it was all she had to keep her warm. So she did what she had to do

to go get her mother her treats. The cold wind whipped across her face as she hopped down the sidewalk to the store.

The little girl made her way through the crowded convenience store. The usual morning rush of customers was there buying coffee and cigarettes.

This time, Chanel remembered her mother's change as she left. She had taken a whipping from her wheelchair-bound mother before; her mother still had such precision and dedication even in her weakness. The second grader didn't want to experience it again. She readied herself to cross the busy street going back to the apartment. Chanel always hated that part. She folded down the opening of the brown paper bag and held on tightly to the 10-ounce glass bottle of Coke. When she thought it was safe, like a runner leaping out of the starting blocks in track and field, she sprang forward off and lunged into the street.

Within a few steps, the child felt a tremendous jolt from her left side, which sent her sailing through the air and landing her on her stomach with a huge thud. Chanel saw the bottle of Coke she had been gripping so tightly only seconds before, roll away from her to the other side of the street. Breathless and confused, she could hear car tires screeching, people yelling and a stampede of footsteps heading in her direction. She had been hit by a car, a big blue station wagon to be exact. With the side of her face hard pressed against the cold concrete road, and gravel digging into her soft cheek, she looked upward at the sky then her eyes moved passed the blue front end of the vehicle. The only thing she could think to say before slipping away into unconsciousness was, "Mama is going to kill me if that Coke bottle breaks."

Chanel was able to tell the paramedics she lived in apartment #509 across the street before waking up an hour later in the hospital, completely numb on her left side.

"Am I paralyzed?" she asked out loud not knowing whether she was alone in the room or not.

"No, sugar you're not paralyzed" said a familiar voice as sweet as iced tea. It was her grandmother, Nannie. Aunt Juanita was there too. "You are banged up pretty bad though."

"Where is my mama?" Chanel asked in concern. "Is she mad at me?"

"Your mama is home and, no, she's not mad at you," Juanita answered. "Your daddy is on his way, to come see about you."
One of her tiny baby teeth was knocked out by the impact. She could feel the empty space with her tongue. She had a broken rib, and a few more scratches and scrapes to match the ones from the car wreck, but she thought she was okay. Her father spent two nights in the hospital with her, but it was all too much for him. His wife lies crippled at home from an awful car crash, with little to no ability to care for herself or their children. Now this with Chanel. He couldn't handle the shape his family was in.

Between the car accident and now Chanel, for Joe leaving seemed like the most convenient option for him at the time. So that's exactly what he did. He left within days of Chanel's accident. Their mother did the best she could and tried to make life as normal as possible, but she often took her frustration out on the older girls. Name calling was common and it only added fuel to the blazing fire of low self-worth Chanel had already been experiencing. "Who would want to go back to that kind of pain?" a daydreaming Chanel asked herself as she looked out of the bedroom window of her new home. This new life in California was looking more and more enticing; she could reinvent herself and have an entirely different feeling about her life. She just hoped her mom would fall in love with it too.

CHAPTER THREE

The first item on Kathy's agenda for settling into the new California life was finding a church. She found one about a mile away from their new house. This was a big step for them. Back in Texas, the family visited a select few churches, but never really grew any roots with any of them. Their father never attended with them.

Things started out a little rocky at Bridgewood Baptist at first. Chanel was shy and always intimidated by meeting new people, especially other kids. Most of the kids had grown up with each other and they didn't allow outsiders into their circles easily. Plus, Chanel had a problem with asserting herself because of the festering self-esteem issues she faced. She tried diligently to suppress the agony she felt from the rejection of her father and the daily criticism from her mother. Chanel thought she was criticized more than her siblings were. She always tried to please her mother, but nothing seemed to turn off the painful words.

The church was very small and mostly run down. It had once been a general store, so you can imagine the look and size. Despite the size of the church, the service was captivating. Unlike any other preacher the girls had known, Pastor Clark could keep their attention.

"We like coming to this church, Mama," Ericka said after the second week.

"Yeah, it's better than Stonewall," young Monique agreed.

"Really? Why is that?" their mother asked.

"Cause we don't fall asleep here like we did at Stonewall."

Kathy laughed.

The small family sat in the back of the church near the exit every Sunday. It wasn't easy making it to a 7:15 a.m. Sunday service on time, but the space in the back allowed for easy maneuvering of Monique's wheelchair. At home, she used crutches, but for convenience on Sunday, they opted for the wheelchair.

Chanel wasn't as impressed as her sisters were with their new church at first. She felt like a freak every time her family walked in. Even though she only recalled one time ever going to church with Joe, when they went to his adoptive mother's funeral, it seemed to her that every family at this church had a father with them, except hers. Monique's wheelchair didn't make things any easier. Everyone stared when they walked into the sanctuary and continued to gape when they packed the chair & Monique back into the car when service was over. So when the time came to interact with their peers at Bridgewood, Chanel's goal was to stay out of the spotlight.

Sunday school was the worst. Chanel couldn't hide behind Kathy, Ericka, or even Monique's wheelchair for that matter. Autumn Turner was her first Sunday school teacher. Sister Turner, as the kids called her, was as short as the 11-year-olds in her class. She had long shiny brown hair and wore bifocal glasses with a red frame. Chanel trembled at the thought of Sister Turner calling on her in class to read a passage of scripture. Even when Chanel didn't raise her hand to volunteer, Sister Turner still called on her every single Sunday.

"I'm sorry, what's your name again sweetheart?" Sister Turner would ask.

"Chanel," she whispered.

"Chanel, what?" the teacher asked, as she cupped her ear.

"Chanel Banks."

"Okay, Chanel Banks, would you like to read St. John, chapter 3, verse 16?" Sister Turner invited her.

"No ma'am." Chanel responded timidly.

The rest of the class erupted with laughter, and all Chanel wanted to do was cry.

Not to be outsmarted, Sister Turner replied, "Well, let me rephrase that. Chanel, please read St. John chapter 3, verse 16 out loud."

Chanel hated Sister Turner and Bridgewood Baptist, and it only got worse.

After a year had gone by, Kathy told the girls they had to join the youth choir. Chanel was absolutely terrified at the prospect of singing alongside strangers, even though she and Ericka had always enjoyed singing around the house.

Not only would she have to sing in front an audience, but she'd have to sing next to the kids that she was convinced didn't even like her.

Rehearsals were on Tuesday evening at 4 o clock, and every time Chanel hoped Kathy would forget. Somehow Ericka had friends, so she sat by them. Chanel took her position in the far left corner of the front row in the choir stand, right behind the microphones. Oddly, she wasn't trying to avoid being heard, but rather being seen. If she could, she would sit in the back row, but anyone with a little church upbringing knows that the back rows of the choir stand are generally reserved for the tenors and baritones.

Mr. Crockett was the director for the choir. Not more than 25 years old himself, he was very skinny with a goatee. He wore his hair in a high-top fade like "Kid" from the 90s rap group, Kid 'N Play. There was a lot of playing and very little focus from this group of kids for a while, but he managed to whip the teens into shape. Chanel's shell was finally cracked when Mr. Crockett selected her to lead a song the choir planned to sing during the Youth Conference. She got so much positive feedback from the director and her peers, it really helped boost her ever fading confidence that life at Bridgewood changed for Chanel after that solo; she made friends and finally enjoyed going to the church. Choir became her refuge and California was beginning to feel like home. Not only did she want to go to choir practice, but she looked forward to Sunday services, youth meetings and even vacation bible school. Chanel discovered that her first love was singing praises and worshiping God, which made her feel good. For the first time, Chanel felt good about herself.

She needed the feeling like she needed oxygen - especially since Kathy never really did anything to make Chanel feel special. It seemed, in fact, like her intentions were to convince Chanel that she wasn't special. Since Ericka was the oldest, she always got first dibs on just about everything: clothes, shoes, birthday bashes. Monique was the baby, and like most families, she was catered to most of her life.

The year Ericka turned 13, Kathy threw her a big birthday celebration in the backyard of their house. She invited all of her friends. There was music, dancing and party games. Some of Ericka's friends even stayed overnight for a sleepover. When Chanel's birthday followed 3 months later, she hoped for similar sentiments from their mother. The morning of, Kathy left the house in a hurry.

"I will be back in a couple of hours," Kathy informed her children. Chanel assumed her rush had something to do with her birthday.

"Yes, ma'am," Chanel responded anxiously, hoping Kathy wouldn't let her down. She spent the rest of the morning speculating what her mom had planned. Hours went by. When she finally arrived back at home at 6:00 p.m., Chanel was dressed and prepared for anything, to go anywhere. She greeted Kathy outside in the driveway.

"Hey mama," she smiled. "You finally made it back."

"Yep, I'm back," Kathy agreed. "What have y'all been doing all day?"
"Just watching tv," Chanel answered, following her mother into the house.
"Well, I did stop by the store to get you something for your birthday."

So, no birthday party, the 12-year-old thought, but Chanel's heart was still filled with expectation.

Kathy reached into her purse and pulled out a pack of grape flavored Now-or-Laters candy, handed them to her daughter and said, "Happy Birthday."

Chanel was crushed. She waited all day for a pack of candy? She could barely mutter a response of appreciation when Kathy reminded her to share her candy, her birthday gift, with her sisters. That same year, Monique enjoyed cupcakes Kathy brought to her school to share with her class. It's no wonder Chanel was so devastated. No kid could feel special after a year like that.

Over time, things started to change at home. Kathy started seeing someone about a year after moving to California, and was planning to marry him. Everyone called him "JP", short for John Paul. He was a little old-fashioned, but a likable person. He owned his own business and seemed to make Kathy happy.

Chanel really didn't know how to take the news. She had started to take solace in things remaining the way they were- her, her mom, and her sisters. She tried to reason, "Maybe having a step dad won't be so bad." JP was a good, hardworking man. But he was short, with a creamy chocolate complexion. It would be difficult for Chanel to pass him off to her friends as her real father, considering a light brown complexion and caramel colored eyes were a slight contradiction of him. The young girl always despised the fact that she had inherited all of her biological father's physical features. Handsome or not, she loathed everything about herself that even remotely resembled him. But eventually Chanel began to see the upside - at least their mom had someone else to focus on, and just maybe she would lay off the insults targeted toward her and her sisters.

JP mostly came to visit in the evenings, but he never came inside the house. He picked up Kathy, or waited outside in his truck until she came home for their date. Chanel couldn't tell if Kathy was just being protective of her girls, or if she wanted to keep JP all to herself. The idea of a blended family was growing on Chanel, but it was hard to imagine, considering JP's kids never came with him to visit. His daughter was grown, but his son was a year behind Chanel and attended the same junior high school as she did. Sometimes her friends would tease her when they would see John Paul II at school.

"There's your brother," they would tease.

"He's not my brother. Stop playing" Chanel shouted back. It wasn't that she didn't want a brother or even a stepbrother, she just didn't know him.

A little more time went by and it was time for her mom to marry JP. The wedding went off without a hitch. It was a quick, uneventful ceremony at the church, after Bible study. JP's younger sister joined them for the ceremony. There was no reception, but the family went to dinner afterwards.

Days before the wedding, their future stepdad found a new house for the new found family. It was very nice, a far cry from that old tacky rambler back in Texas. It was two stories, with a two-car garage and had a beautiful sunroom. Each of the girls would finally have her own room, but they all had to share one bathroom upstairs. JP and Kathy's master suite was downstairs, just off the living room. Since there were two levels, Kathy decided the family now needed two telephone lines. This setup worked well for Chanel and Ericka, who had always wanted their own phone number to talk to their friends privately. It was perfect!

Chanel had just started high school when Kathy and JP got married. She looked forward to exploring her new found freedom, but she wasn't the only one. Ericka was starting to act out in more ways than one. Her conduct went beyond the typical teenage outbursts. Finally, things became so tense between Ericka and their mother that Ericka left. She was either thrown out or had decided to run away. Prior to Ericka's departure, the family tried counseling and other interventions, but she and Kathy continued to bump heads.

Chanel thought that by finally having a father figure around, they would begin to function more like a family unit. The reality was anything but. Sadly, it was more like JP married Kathy to be with Kathy, not the kids; the new couple was living their lives separately from the girls. When Ericka left, Kathy made Chanel her younger sibling's primary caregiver and she grew to resent her little sister for it. She wasn't allowed to participate in school activities and other activities like other kids her age because of the added responsibilities at home. She was home immediately after school every day to get Monique off of the school bus, help her with homework and then do her own. Chanel was responsible for combing Monique's hair in the morning and making sure she was ready for school every day. She basically took over Kathy's job of being Monique's mother.

It was not like anything Chanel had hoped for. The blended family rarely did anything together. Besides the Sunday morning drive to church, there was absolutely no quality time spent getting to know each other. JP and Kathy would go to dinner most nights and leave the girls at home. In fact, their relationship with their stepfather was so formal that even after they married, the girls referred to JP as "Mr. Mackey." The teenager's nagging desire for a strong family life plagued her the rest of her life.

JP was not a bad guy. He worked hard and didn't drink like Joe, but it was strange living with a man in the house. Especially since he was still basically a stranger. As much as Chanel wanted a father, she was most comfortable at home when her stepdad wasn't there. Maybe that's why Ericka started having so many issues.

Not long after Ericka left living with her family, she was pregnant and had a son two months before graduating high school. She named the baby Jeremiah. Chanel hoped that Jeremiah would help bridge the huge gap growing between Ericka and their mom. He did for a while, but they eventually grew further apart. Chanel couldn't be more thrilled about becoming an aunt. She was in love with Jeremiah and he loved her too. Ironically, her nephew was so special to her that their closeness eventually created a wedge between the sisters. As the baby grew, so did the tension. Ericka made one questionable choice after another about her life, and this time, those poor decisions were affecting her son

When Jeremiah was one, the family experienced something that affected them all. On a cold day in January, just after kids returned to school from Christmas break. Chanel got off of the school bus a block from her house, as she walked closer she could see that there was a fire truck on her street near her house. The lights from the big trucks were flashing violently. Kathy's car seemed to be dangerously close to a ditch and the driver's side door was opened wide. From a distance, Chanel thought her mother had been in some minor accident, but finally she could see it wasn't a wreck at all. The second floor of the house was on fire.

Chanel's dream home was going up in smoke right before her eyes. It was like something right out of the movies. She was in such disbelief that she hardly remembered what happened immediately after this event. Her step father had been home sick that day when the fire broke out. Thankfully, no one else was home or hurt in the fire, but their lives were once again changed. Ericka had moved out and Kathy had sent Monique to stay in an independent living school that would help her learn life skills.

The night of the fire, Chanel stayed with her best friend, Charlotte, and her family. Chanel thought it would only be one night, since the damage didn't seem to be significant from the outside, but one night turned into weeks. She was shuffled around for months. No one thought about the emotional impact these events had on Chanel. Maybe it was the brave front she put on when her mom came around, but Chanel was crumbling inside. She was just beginning to come into her own as a young woman; she had finally begun to get the attention of boys she went to high school with and wanted to date and have visitors come by the house. Now there was not a home to bring them to. Kathy had one big rule. She could not go out with anyone her mother did not know. That fire couldn't have happened at worst time for the teenager.

Living with her friend, Charlotte was awesome. She had a twin brother named Brian and the three of them cut up and argued as if they were all siblings. One day, the three of them were discussing their plans to go to the Sadie Hawkins dance at Charlotte and Chanel's school. Brian, who was a known trouble maker was forced out of tradition high school and banished to an alternative school, but he wanted to go so he could show off his new "high yellow" girlfriend to his old friends. High yellow was a southern nickname usually reserved for that fairer complexion of the black population.

"We have to find a ride to the dance, man, especially since your Mustang is still in the shop, Chanel, AGAIN!" Charlotte joked.

"I know. I hate that car." Chanel agreed. Kathy had bought a very used Mustang which she tried to pass off has a gift for Chanel once she got her driver's license, but it was really meant for Ericka seeing as how the keys went right into her hands days after purchasing it. By the time her big sister was tired of it and Chanel finally got a chance to get behind the wheel, it was so rundown and unreliable it was more of an embarrassment than a confidence booster.

"Brian, how are you and Amber getting there?" questioned Chanel

"Mom said I could take her car," Brian replied confidently.

Laughing out loud, Charlotte said, "Boy, you're crazy. Mom ain't stupid. She won't let you use her car to be toting your hookers around in it."

"I swear she did. Ask her," Brian contended.

"Well, if she did then you have to take us too!" Chanel incited.

"What? Hell, no. You must be crazy. I'm not taking y'all nowhere with me," Brian gasped in frustration.

"I bet you will," Charlotte chimed in.
And just as she had said so, he did just that.

The four teenagers rode together the night of the dance. Brian hated every minute of the car ride. Charlotte and Chanel did their best to humiliate him in front of his girlfriend, and he tried to leave the dance without them twice that night. Chanel always treasured their friendship because she got the comfort and love she'd been seeking from home. Ironically, Kathy trusted the twins more than any of Chanel's other friends, but she got into more mischievous behavior with Brian and Charlotte than anyone else.

After living with the twins and their mother for a few weeks, Chanel was forced to live in a one bedroom house with Ericka, Jeremiah, and Ericka's husband, Keith. The two had gotten married on a whim at the courthouse about month after they met. The family was first introduced to Keith two weeks after the wedding.

Chanel was so uncomfortable there; she felt imprisoned. It was in a crummy part of town and she had no friends around. The place was small; she had no privacy and to make matters worse, Ericka didn't even have a telephone. There was never any food to eat. Chanel was miserable. It was one of the most frustrating times in her life. She lived with Ericka and her family for eight long months, and she detested every day of it - mostly because she felt like she was intruding.

It wasn't all, Keith did teach her how to drive and helped get her license when she lived there. Maybe Chanel wouldn't have felt like she was trapped if she could've actually use the 1981 Mustang Kathy bought. The paint job was a faded powder blue, with matching cloth interior. It was rusted in spots on the exterior. The seatbelts were broken and the radio only worked if she hit a pothole in the road, or drove over a railroad track. Both the air conditioning and heat were shot. The car spent more time in the repair shop than on the road. That was the condition Kathy bought it in and Ericka only punished it more. At this point, the car and Chanel's life sucked.

As if things couldn't get any worse, Ericka and Keith got evicted. So, by the summer, Chanel was sleeping on the front office floor of her stepdad's construction company. Kathy and JP went to live there after a temporary stint in a hotel while they figured out what they were going to do about the house. The office did have an extra room off the main building, which her parents used as a bedroom for now. There was a bathroom, but no tub, only a toilet and sink. Chanel had to bathe in an old-fashioned washtub every night. She was realizing how good she had it before; Ericka's run down place now looked like the Hyatt from her perspective. It would be two years before the house was semi-restored and her mother and step-father moved back in, but by then, Chanel was living away at college.

Until then, Chanel's escape was her part-time job. She was hired on the spot when she filled out an application at a grocery store called Ralph's. It wasn't much money, but it made her really proud. She could earn her own money, which came in handy - especially going into her senior year of high school. Knowing her mother wasn't going to do all the special things that came along with being a senior, she made sure she made a way for herself. She saved to buy her own class ring and senior supplies like graduation invitations and pictures.

Kathy eventually rented another apartment for Ericka and her family. Apparently, she felt sorry for the young couple trying to care for Jeremiah, while expecting another baby. The apartment wasn't far from the home that burned, so Chanel felt a little more at home when she learned she had to move in with Ericka again. This time she at least had her own room. More specifically, she shared the second bedroom with her 1 year old nephew. But at least she had a bath tub to bathe in.

That fall, Chanel started her senior year in high school. She had changed schools a couple of times in order to escape the high school drama of her previous school. Chanel was never a part of the "in crowd." She had a small group of friends from every clique, but for some reason she always stayed on the "mean girls' radar everywhere she went. She was constantly bullied for wearing hand-me-downs, none of which were fashionable. The mostly shy teen was also picked on for wearing knock-off Adidas sneakers and carrying counterfeit Dooney & Burke handbags. She never knew how the girls could tell, but they always knew. There was even a rumor about her sleeping around and getting pregnant, which was especially troubling considering she was still a virgin and didn't have a boyfriend to speak of. She was looking forward to a fresh start; new school, new clothes and a new haircut. The only thing not fresh were her wheels. The Mustang was down most of the summer and it was still down, but Chanel couldn't bear the thought of riding the school bus as a senior, so she presented her plan to her mother.

"Mama, do I have to ride the bus to school this year if I can get a ride?" she asked nervously.

"A ride? A ride with who?" Kathy asked.
"With Devon. Devon Sanders," she replied.

It took a lot of courage for the teenager to even fix her mouth to ask such a question, but Chanel was fed up with all the restrictions put on her. Kathy's answer was usually 'no' when it came to anything she wanted to do. Chanel felt like she was continuously punished for how Ericka mishandled responsibility when she was her age, and she didn't like it. It wasn't fair because she and Ericka were two completely different types of people.

"I don't know who Devon is." Kathy insisted.

"You know her from church. She's Deacon Sanders' youngest daughter and she's a senior too."

"Hmm," Kathy hesitated. "Well, let me find out from her parents if she has a driver's license first, and I will let you."

Finally, a victory of sorts for the teen. Kathy was always more comfortable letting Chanel do things that involved anyone from their church. She never thought she would hear an easy yes, let alone maybe from her mother. So this was good to her. Now, if Kathy would only agree to let her date! Chanel wanted to go out with guys her own age now more than ever.

The boy who king of her heart since the first day of 9th grade was Dawson Ayers. He was very smart, a great dancer and well-liked in school. She admired that the most. She'd abandoned him when she left for a new school, but they were still in touch and good friends. That was the problem. They were just friends. When they went to the same school, Dawson always acknowledged Chanel and made her think he liked her by his flirting, but he would never ask her out. Guys like him always had a girlfriend, but Chanel wanted to make sure he knew she was still an option and interested every chance she could. One day she concocted a plan to make sure Dawson had no other choice but to notice her on a daily basis. She and her locker mate staged a fight in the hallway before class one morning.

"See, I know Dawson doesn't share his locker with anyone. So we have to pretend as if we're having a big argument. You can start throwing my things out and onto the floor so Dawson will see, and maybe step in, "Chanel explained her conniving plan.

"Okay, okay," her friend agreed. "I got it. Here he comes." As Dawson rounded the corner the fake quarrel ensued.

"I'm really getting sick and tired of you telling my business to everybody in school, Chanel," she yelled

"What business? You don't have any business to tell," Chanel jabbed back.

The two girls shouted and threw books at each other dramatically as their peers, including Dawson, looked on. The fake fight ended with her formal locker buddy telling her to find someone else to pair up with.

"Don't even try to play dumb. See I was tryin' to help you out by letting you keep your raggedy shit in my locker, but I don't share with snakes and that's just what you are, □" her friend said.

Her partner in crime was playing her role a little too well. She was so convincing that even Chanel started to believe it. So she had to cut things off. Besides, the whole 10th grade was watching the event unfold.

"I won't even tell you what I think of you and your locker. I'll just take my raggedy shit and leave," Chanel snapped.
But, before she could reach for anything, her co-star commenced to send her geometry book sailing through the air, landing with a loud smack on the cold floor.
Under her breath, Chanel said, "Thanks girl."

Dawson had to have heard all the commotion going on. He was only five lockers away, with a ring side seat. Chanel gathered her things and casually waltzed over to the person with the locker next to Dawson's locker and asked if she could store her things there until she got a new locker assignment. It was all apart of the master plan.

He said, "Naw, I'm sorry. I'm already sharing with two other people. I don't want anyone else invading my space. It would be too much, but, Dawson is rolling solo, huh?"

Dawson glanced over looking into Chanel's caramel colored eyes when she asked, "Is that true, Dawson? You don't have a locker mate?"

"No, I don't. It's just me," he said as very smoothly. Dawson was so sweet. Every word he spoke rolled off his lips like milk chocolate.

"Well, do you mind if I keep my things in your locker for a while then?" Chanel knew he would say yes. He was just that type of guy.

"I guess its okay, I don't mind., Dawson replied.

And just like that, she had gotten close to him. The plan worked! If only the rest of her life could go so smoothly when she made plans.

Chanel was too old for those sorts of childish games now. After all, she'sa senior now, and she wanted to do all the things seniors in high school did, but with Dawson. Until then, she just tried to fit in at her new school.

Making friends was easy. Most of the kids had gone to junior high with her, so there were connections in place already, making the transition fairly smooth. Plus, Ralph's was minutes from the school and it was a popular hangout for the school football team after practices.

Chanel was a cashier, which meant she would get a lot of attention from the guys when they came in to her job. Her manager, a middle-aged gay man who wore way too much cologne, would always conveniently rush over to take over her register when the team showed up. He preferred barking out orders to Chanel in hopes to distract her from flirting back with the boys, but that only freed her up to hand out more than a fair share of free whoppers and smiles to her new admirers.

One guy was so smitten with Chanel, he came back inside the store after the rest of the team left, just so he could ask her for her telephone number. He was cute, but he wasn't Dawson. Their romance lasted about as long as it took for Chanel to find out she wasn't his first choice.

By Homecoming, Chanel decided it was time to go on her first real date. No one, including Dawson, was expressing interest in taking her to the dance, so she decided her first date would be with a guy she asked out. So she decided to ask Emmanuel. He was 6'3", a receiver on their high school football team, and was as handsome as boys her age came. It took a few days for Chanel to build up the nerve to talk to him, let alone ask him to go out with her. She didn't even have the okay from Kathy that she could go out with a boy either. But that was the least of her concern.

Chanel had four classes with this guy, but she waited until 4th period that day to spring her question on him. She got to class early and sat in her regular seat in the front row. She wanted to make sure she caught him as he walked in, not wanting to risk the possibility of any of his stupid friends interrupting their conversation.

Chanel watched nervously as he walked into the classroom and headed closer to her desk. She blurted out, "Hey Emmanuel. How are you?" as she batted her eyes and smiled.

Emmanuel smiling back, stopped in his tracks, likely in shock, since Chanel never really spoke to him before. He said, "I'm doing well, Chanel. How are you?"

"I'm great. I have a question for you," she started. He looked intrigued.

"Do you have a date for the Homecoming dance?" she asked, as her mouth grew dry and her heart seemed as if it was beating through her shirt.

Emmanuel's smile grew about two feet wide as he quickly replied, "No, I don't. Why do you ask?"

"Because I was wondering if you would like to be my date?" She winced as the words rolled past her lips. She couldn't believe she had said it, but she did. She waited for the rejection.

Without hesitation, he replied, "Sure. I would like that. Can I have your number so we can talk about it?"

"Yes." Chanel smiled back in disbelief. He didn't reject her. Her smile was about five feet wide, but all she could think about was how she would tell Kathy.

So, she went home and mustard up the same courage to ask her mom-maybe a little more this time. But she pulled all of her tricks out of the hat for this one. Kathy initially gave her a hard time about going, but eventually gave in, despite not meeting Emmanuel until the night he picked her up. The dance was nice and so was Chanel's date. She hoped Emmanuel would try to kiss her goodbye that evening, but he remained a complete gentleman. He even took her by to meet his parents and took pictures before driving her home. He was the first guy to bring Chanel home to meet his parents, and would be the only one for a long time.

Kathy and Ericka were still fighting. Their mother and JP eventually moved into Ericka's apartment with Chanel, and as the lease holder, she made Ericka and her family to move out, including their newest addition, another baby boy they named Andrew. Unfortunately, they had to. This only caused even more divide amongst them all.

When spring came around, Chanel applied for college. She always knew she would go away to school, but she wanted to get away now more than ever, especially since she didn't have a stable place to live. She would've went anywhere or studied anything just to get away.

Chanel has dreamt of studying law since the 7th grade. Since there wasn't anyone really guiding her decision or anything else, she put all of her eggs into one basket and never requested information from any other schools. The acceptance letter to the University of San Diego came just weeks after sending her enrollment and financial aid applications off. Chanel hoped that Kathy or Joe had been secretly putting away money for their girls' education, but that couldn't have been any further from the truth.

If she was going to go to college, it was going to be financed by Uncle Sam. At least her paychecks were coming in handy to cover senior supplies. Cap and gown, senior book and pictures and even her class ring, Chanel always footed the bill. The ring was the first piece of genuine jewelry she 'd ever bought, and that made the young woman proud.

CHAPTER FOUR

High school graduation came with much excitement. Chanel didn't struggle with any classes. She had managed to finish high school as number 25 in her class of 210, with a 3.8 overall grade point average. More than anything, she was thrilled to be moving away from home. She had no reason to think her family was proud of her. As they never have been before. Even though she was the first to go away to college, her accomplishment didn't garner the attention she expected it would.

Her father ignored her invitation to the graduation ceremony. Though she'd mailed the invitation well in advance, he didn't even call to say he couldn't make it. The family didn't offer any celebratory event, no graduation festivity, not a party or even a celebration dinner. That day was one of the most important days of her life and by the time it was over, Chanel was left wondering what all her hard work was for. She was bitter about it for a while. Why wouldn't she be? Kathy and JP didn't even stick around after the ceremony to take pictures with her. This hurt Chanel, considering the family, including grandparents, had gone to dinner after Ericka's big day. She expected even a fraction of the attention she got.

A call from Aunt Teddy days after the graduation gave Chanel a ray of inspiration. Teddy was Kathy and Juanita's baby sister. Her real name was Teresa, but she changed it to Teddy in the eighties. She was in the military and had told the family she was a lesbian after she came home from boot camp.

"Hey, Nel. How are you doing?" Aunt Teddy was the only one in the family who still called Chanel by her childhood nickname.

"I'm doing well, Aunt Teddy. I'm just glad to be finished with high school." Chanel replied.

"I'm sorry I missed the graduation, but I couldn't get the time off from my part-time job at the hotel. I really wanted to be there," She said.

"I know you did. Don't worry about it. Thank you for the money you sent. It was my only gift," Chanel said with a sad face.

"Aww you're welcome, baby. Hey, I was wondering, how would you like to come out here to work before you go off to school?" Teddy asked hoping she'd come where she lived in Atlanta.

"Well, I still have my job at Ralph's . I was planning to work there through the summer." Chanel liked working with her friends. They had a good time.

"I know, but the Summer Olympics are being hosted here. You can make a lot more money out here than there. Why don't you think about coming down?" She asked again with more motivation in her voice.

"That's true," Chanel agreed. "I will let you know after I talk to my mother, and thanks, for offering," She replied.

"Okay, talk to her and call me tonight." Teddy replied.

She had a good point. Chanel certainly could make more money working an event like that. The Olympics is huge. She could likely have a nice bit of cash saved for a few school expenses.

Maybe Teddy is right, she thought. I should go. Her only hesitation was that she didn't always get along with Teddy's "friends" or her 15-year-old cousin Tiffany, Teddy's daughter. She was spoiled rotten and Chanel couldn't stand it, or her.

"I can make it work though," Chanel was optimistic. "It will only be a couple of months and I'll be at work most of the time anyway. I'll call her back and say yes after work."

Chanel was surprised that Kathy went along with it, as she never really seemed to want to help Chanel get ahead. But, things didn't quite work out as planned when she got there. Everyone else in America had the same idea; go to Atlanta and make a small fortune selling over priced goods during the summer games or land a big time temporary job downtown in the epicenter of the event. Chanel spent the entire summer filling out job applications all over the city. When she finally landed a position in a record store one month before her classes started at USD, she couldn't get her schedule to work out so she could make the extra money she was hoping for. Sam Goody had hired so much temporary help, there weren't enough hours to go around.

She called her manager every day, trying to get on the schedule.

"Hi, it's Chanel again. I'm just letting you know I'm available to come in today or any day this week if you need me to," She would say every time.

"Okay, Chanel. I got you down," the store manager responded. "I will try to fit you in the day after tomorrow."

They frequently gave Chanel the run around. She hated appearing desperate, but she kind of was at this point.

I should have never come out here,Chanel thought, as she hiked up the steep hill toward home in the heat. Aunt Teddy's place was just off a main highway, and sometimes Chanel would walk to find work. Besides, the little cash she had was being eaten away daily due to her traveling on the MARTA to job search. She'd been on so many wild goose chases searching for work on failed promises. It was useless.

To help get her mind off her unemployment woes, Teddy suggested she, Chanel, and Tiffany hang out at Centennial Park for Chanel's birthday.
"I know you haven't had a chance to do much but job hunt since you've been here. You need to enjoy yourself." Teddy said. "Let's go downtown to Centennial Park on Friday to celebrate. It's your big 18th!"

"Oooh that sounds fun," Tiffany chimed in. "I've been wanting to go down there, too."

Downtown was a literal zoo with all the Olympic traffic. She's experienced her fair share of overheated, overcrowded trains and plazas filled with the fragrant funk of national and international tourists.

"Let's just go out to someplace nice in Buckhead to eat," she offered instead.

"Ok, that's fine too. Whatever you want. It's your birthday," Teddy obliged.

On Friday night, the three of them went out as planned. It wasn't exactly how Chanel dreamed she would ring in her independence, but it was better than what she was accustomed to back home with her mother and sisters. She remembered for her sweet 16, she and Charlotte walked a mile and a half to Dairy Queen and ate Oreo blizzards. When she got home, Kathy and JP had left her a sink full of dirty dishes to wash and a happy birthday card on the steps leading upstairs to her room. At least Teddy and Tiffany made her feel special, even if it was only for one night.

After they made it home, sometime in the early morning, Chanel was awakened to someone calling her name. She thought she was dreaming until she felt a jolt in her right arm, which turned out to be Aunt Teddy shaking her.

"Chanel, Chanel, wake up! Girl, you saved our lives," Teddy shouted. "You saved us!"

"What…what are you talking about?" Chanel slurred her speech.

She had dozed off on the tacky zebra print chaise in Tiffany's purple and white polka dotted room. "What do you mean?" She asked as she was waking up more and more.

"Somebody blew up the park. They blew up Centennial Park," Teddy exaggerated somewhat.

The night before, someone had planted three homemade pipe bombs in a backpack under a bench near the concert stage at the park.

"It's all over the news," Teddy told her. The two of them hurried to the living room to see more of the report. Tiffany had not flinched during all the commotion. She was still asleep in her bed.

"One woman has died and hundreds reportedly injured," the announcer said.

"That could have been one of us if we'd gone down there like I wanted," Teddy sympathized. "Girl, you're my hero!" Teddy laughed sarcastically, hugging her niece.

"Yeah, I guess," Chanel said proudly. "I guess I kind of am."

Unfortunately, the Park bombing was the only excitement in Atlanta that summer. In all, Chanel earned about $200 working at the record store, but she spent $100 of it on the bus ticket Kathy made her pay for to get home. Forty-nine hours and eight bus transfers later, she was finally home. It was early August by then, and Chanel couldn't wait to go away to college. Like any college freshman, she was enthusiastic about her future and was sure she would take over the world someday.

When they made it to campus, Kathy dumped Chanel off at the dormitory, showing no emotion at all. This lack of interest set the tone for Chanel's journey through her undergraduate studies.

Chanel was left with one oversized suitcase, an iron, a set of sheets, and a blanket; all of which was still perfumed by the scent of smoke left over from the house fire the year before. Chanel was embarrassed when she saw the TV/VCR combo, refrigerator, and microwave her roommate had set up to make her space feel like home. There was even a cute blue and white valance in the skinny window to match this girl's bedding. She even had pictures mounted on the walls.

Good grief, what time did this girl get here? Chanel thought. Her family thought of everything.

In their defense, Chanel was the first member of her family to ever go away to college. No one could have predicted what an undergraduate living on campus would need. But she was sure no one cared that much to even think much about it.

Chanel had to figure out everything on her own. She let out a big sigh and began the task of unpacking and dressing her scanty side of the room.

Chanel's roommate didn't return that first night, so their first encounter was delayed a while. She spent the rest of the day alone, trying to interpret the course catalog.

Chanel heard from her hair dresser that LaTonya would be attending USD too.So, in the morning, she ventured to the 6th floor to meet up with her. Tonya's family were members of Bridgewood too, when the girls were much younger. They hadn't kept in touch, but any friendly face is welcomed in a new setting with no other friends.

"So, what's your major?" Chanel asked, as they walked to the cafeteria for breakfast.

"Girl, I don't know. I haven't declared one yet." Tonya remarked. "My mother will be back tomorrow to help me choose my courses and I'll go from there."

Chanel thought it was pretty foolish of Tonya to come all the way to a university and have no idea of what she wanted to do with her life. Chanel had known her passion was law and boasted about it to anyone whether they asked or not.

"Well, I'm going to study law," Chanel voiced proudly. "I'll be in court working side by side with Johnny Cochran someday. You watch."

The girls spent the rest of the morning in the Student Union people watching. It was truly a cultural experience. Students were there from all over the country. It was fun guessing which region of the United States the Timberland boots, gold teeth, two inch-long acrylic nails, or name plated belt buckles came from. And the accents, they were sometimes dumbfounding to match up with a region.

By dinner time, Chanel's roommate had returned.

"Heeeeeyyyy, girl!" she said as she entered the room. "I'm Tori Franklin."She reached out her long arms, not her hands, to pull Chanel in for a hug. Tori was pretty tall for a girl - nearly six feet. She was on the slender side, with long, dark, curly hair.

"Oh! Okay. You're my roommate," Chanel said as her reason to hugging Tori back. "My name is Chanel Banks."

As Tori closed the door behind her, she asked, "When did you get here?"

"I got in yesterday, around noon. I think you had already left," Chanel answered.

"Yeah, my cousin brought me here pretty early. She lives off campus and she had to get her boyfriend's car back to him so he could go to work. I spent the night at their place."

They went through the back and forth dialogue getting to know each other. Tori was very sweet, which made Chanel happy. Her fears of having a roommate from hell were gradually dispelled. They lived in Grant Hall, which had six floors and was classified as a freshman girl's dorm in the Freshman Complex. It was strategically positioned in the very back of the campus, overlooking what appeared to be cattle pasture. There were four rooms assigned to a suite, which meant two people per room andeight people in a suite. Chanel had to share a common area, study section, one shower, one toilet, and two sinks with 7 other girls. It was going to be a challenge for sure. But she would rather this challenge than the one back home with her family.

The male dorm for freshman guys was directly across the courtyard from Grant, and the guys had their own ideas of what would be an appropriate welcome to their female counterparts. That night, the guys decided to put on a strip show in their windows for the young ladies across the yard, and anyone else who wanted to see. They used flashlights to help illuminate their bodies for better viewing. Chanel had never seen a boy's naked body before this. Two of Chanel's suite mates were all too pleased to encourage the boys further by starting a strip show of their own.

So, this is what college is all about? Chanel thought.

Tori's show was interrupted twice by calls from her cousin and mother calling to check on her, to make sure she didn't need anything.

That wouldn't be the only night Chanel and Tori would have to fall asleep to flickering beams of light piercing through their window. Chanel wondered when someone would call to see how she was doing or how she was handling her new found freedom. With all that was going on in the windows, Lord knows somebody needed to.

Abandonment really began to sink in for Chanel when she realized she still owed thousands of dollars for tuition on her billing statement. But she was realistic enough to know no one from her family would be around to help her out. LaTonya's mother was kind enough to stick around and help Chanel through the process of registering for classes. And what she couldn't figure out, the academic advisor squeezed in 10 minutes of direction.

But tuition was a different story all together. Chanel did what any kid would do. She called her mama. Of course, Kathy had already returned home, not once checking in to see how things were going.

"Mama, what are you doing?" Chanel inquired.

"I'm cooking, why?" Kathy replied.

"Well, we got our statements today and I still owe $4,500 on my tuition. If the balance isn't paid in full by Friday, they will delete all of the courses I registered for out of the system." She knew very well Kathy would not sympathize, but what else could she do?
"Where is your financial aid, Chanel? Didn't you apply for financial aid?" Kathy was shouting so loudly into the phone, Chanel was afraid the other students waiting in line for the pay phone behind her would hear the insults Kathy spewed out and would be frightened too.

"I did apply for financial aid because two of the other schools I considered confirmed they have it, but USD hasn't received it yet."

She was sure now that Kathy would turn around and come back to help, or at least make a phone call to someone, anyone. Besides, her child was out there alone, scared, without a clue of what to do next. But Kathy responded in her typical fashion."All I can tell you is, you better get on the Greyhound bus and go to one of those other schools that have your money."

What? Chanel thought in mere disbelief

That's it. Kathy never considered coming back to help Chanel get over this difficult hump. Chanel learned a huge lesson in independence that day. From that moment on, she had to make life happen alone. If she couldn't count on the person who gave birth to her to come to her aid when she was in distress, who else would?

The 18-year-old began considering all of her options at that point.

"Leaving school before I start school won't work," she began. I don't even know if I have enough money to take a bus down to Cal State, was her second thought. Then, of course, there's the military route. Chanel had a terrifying brush with almost joining the Marine Corp. Their recruiters were ready and willing to write a check to pay vulnerable students' tuition, but only if they signed the next four years of their lives over to them.

Chanel was looking for support from all directions when it came to getting her financial aid drama worked out. She found herself in conversation with a 65 year-old, out of shape, gray-haired athletic coach who claimed he had many connections in the financial aid office. He promised her he would do everything he could to get the matter resolved for her. What he really meant though, was that he wanted Chanel to do anything for him to get the matter resolved.

Two days into the headache of trying to get an appointment with a financial aid counselor, Coach Bernie asked Chanel to give him her room telephone number.

"I will call you once I speak to my contact in the financial aid office and I'll let you know when you can come in for a meeting." He said.

"Thanks, Coach. I really appreciate all of your help," Chanel replied, and gladly gave him the number to her dorm room. Her hope was restored. Maybe I won't have to join the military, after all, she thought. She was really naïve and thought it was as simple as that,

When the call came the next day, she was thrilled, but that thrill soon fizzled out.

"Hey, baby girl it's Coach Bernie."

"Hey Coach, how's it going? Did you talk with the counselor for me?" she inquired.

"Well, not yet. He hasn't returned my call yet," the coach muttered. "But in the meantime, I was wondering if you wanted to meet me for ice cream?" he asked. "It will help you get your mind off things."
What am I? 12? Chanel thought. What is ice cream going to do for my tuition?

"Ice cream?" she responded out loud.

"Yeah," the old coach said. "I thought we could get a cone and lick it together."

Suddenly, the idea of joining the military didn't seem to scare Chanel nearly as much as the possibility of being molested by a dirty old man. "Are you serious?" she asked.

"Sure, why not?" He arrogantly replied.

"Naw, that's not going to be a good idea," Chanel responded, and quickly hung up the telephone.

It was a good thing she never mentioned which dormitory she was assigned to, but it wouldn't have been difficult to find out with the Coach's connections and all. Plus, ninety percent of the freshman girls were housed in the same dorm. She eventually got a coveted meeting with a financial aid counselor, who agreed to write her a promissory note. Chanel never saw Coach Bernie again. Terrified, she was hopeful her life would still go according to how she'd dreamed, since she signed an intimidating promissory note instead, to secure her future. It wouldn't be long before she realized she was wrong.

After the drama of paying tuition was over, Chanel was finally able to focus on other things, like meeting people and hanging out. Her life at home had been so restricted, and she hardly knew what to do as a newly liberated woman. Girls were staying out late and inviting boys into their dorm rooms, even though there was a curfew in place and co-ed visits were not allowed for freshmen. It was all new territory to Chanel. She managed to finish high school as a virgin.

Her first night in the dorm, she met two girls from Michigan who were roommates. They were both named Alana; Alana Clark and Alana Drummond. She used the first initial of their last name to distinguish between the two. She stumbled upon their room while searching for another high school classmate. "Where are you from?" Alana C. asked.

"I'm from Texas, but I lived seven years or so in Bakersfield, California. It's just outside of Los Angeles" Chanel replied. "Ever heard of it?"

"Yes, I know where that is," Alana D. responded. "It's a few hours from here, right?"

"Yeah, that's right. What about y"all? Where are y'all from?" Chanel knew they couldn't be from anywhere from down south or the west coast, but she could not pick up on their accent. Plus, they were so well-spoken. Every word they had spoken so far was grammatically correct.

"Saginaw, Michigan, but I was born right here in Cali," Alana D. claimed.

"Cool," she paused. "Well, it's late. Forgive me again for waking y'all." Chanel said. "Here's my room number. If you hear of someone named Ebony Jones, please give her my number."

"Ok, we will," the girls said in unison.

Chanel and her new friends ate every meal together and attended every campus event as a team. They were inseparable. She had a few classes with Alana D., so they chatted often about which guys on campus were the cutest. There was one guy in particular that Chanel really wanted to meet. She didn't know his name at the time, but she was about to find out.

One day before class, Alana D. told Chanel she'd found out some information she would be interested in.

"Hey girl, I have some news for you about that boy."

"What boy?" Chanel questioned.

"You know. The one always wearing that red and white Adidas t-shirt you hate so much, but you think is so cute," She said with a smirk on her face.

Chanel was stunned.

Alana continued, " The one we sat across from Saturday in the café?"

"Oh, my goodness, what did you find out?" Chanel was so anxious.

"Well, his name is Langston, and he's from Philly," she said

"How did you find out?" Chanel marveled.

"Well, I walked right up to him and asked." Alana answered, with a matter-of–fact attitude. Alana D. stood there with her green eyes as big as saucers and her hands on her hips.

"And I got his phone number," she finished.

"What? Wait a minute. Let me get this straight," Chanel tried to rationalize. "You just walked up to a guy you don't even know, asked him his name, where he's from, and he just gave you his phone number?"

"Yes and no," Alana explained. "He did give me his name when

I asked and told me where he's from. He only gave me his phone number when I told him I had a friend who was interested in meeting him."

"You said WHAT?" Chanel yelled. "Oh, my God, you did?"

"I did," Alana smiled confidently. "And he's expecting you to call him after dinner tonight so the two of you can meet."

"MEET! Meet where? You can't be serious," Chanel asked in disbelief. "This is way too much."
She hadn't been this forward with a guy since her high school Homecoming date with Emmanuel, and that was nearly way too tough. The thought of trying to start a conversation with this boy was more than intimidating, it was terrifying. This guy was from the east coast. He was probably smarter and savvier than Chanel was. She was afraid she would not only look like an idiot, but she would sound like one too.

She was so anxious when she made that initial call. It took her two days to build up the courage to dial the number. It was actually kind of fun watching him on the yard, having no clue she was the person Alana D. had told him about. Her voice cracked, when he answered.

"Hi, may I speak to Langston," Chanel asked, trying not to stutter.

"This is Langston," he responded. Chanel could tell he was smiling.

"Hey Langston, my name is Chanel. A friend of mine, Alana, told you about me the other day."

"Oh yeeeaaah, that's right," he remembered. Chanel was somewhat relieved. "How are you?" he asked. He sounded so smart. She could hardly contain herself.

"I'm doing well. How are things going for you so far?" They had only been in classes a couple of weeks by then, so everything was still kind of fresh.

"I really can't complain. Good, I guess," he said.

They chatted for a couple more minutes with small talk. Chanel kept switching the phone's receiver from one hand to the other because her palms were sweating. Then he asked Chanel to come downstairs and meet him in the lobby of Grant Hall.

"Okay, I can do that. How about in 10 minutes?" Chanel needed time to make herself look presentable. It was Saturday and she'd been in bed in her sweats most of the day. She hadn't even brushed her teeth.

"Sounds good. See you then," Langston replied.
She immediately called Alana. "Girl, get down here to my room right now. I'm about to go meet this guy in the lobby."

"Ooooooo, I can't wait!!!" Alana exclaimed over the phone. "I'm on my way."
Ten minutes turned into 20 as the girls tried to piece together something simple, but cute for her to wear. Chanel didn't want to over do it, but still wanted to make a good impression. They came up with a pair of white shorts (even though it was well past Labor Day) and a cute blue and white tee with Donald Duck on the front. Chanel was hoping Langston would see she was still a kid at heart and liked to have fun.

He was patiently waiting there, sitting on a sofa in the lobby. Their eyes met as soon as she stepped off the elevator. Langston stood up from his seat, knowing she had to be Chanel. He met her half way as he walked over with a big, bright smile, probably just relieved Chanel wasn't an ugly duckling like the one on her t-shirt. Langston was about 5'10, with dark chocolate coated skin, and jet black wavy hair. Of course, he was wearing that stupid red & white Adidas t-shirt Chanel hated so much, but he looked good anyway. He was her Blair Underwood.

The two of them decided to take a quick walk down to the lake on campus. It was always so nice there. They talked a little more before heading their separate ways for dinner. Dinner was an easy out - just in case the two didn't connect.

It was an unusually mild, slightly windy evening; the temperature is always scorching hot, even at that time of day. Chanel was just thankful she didn't have to fight back sweat bullets as she discussed her hometown and academic plans with that chocolate treat sitting next to her, on the stone benches, across from the lake.

"So where are you from?" she asked.

"I grew up in Philadelphia, but I graduated from high school in Alaska. I'm an only child. It's just me and my parents. .
"Alaska? Are you serious?" She laughed. Chanel didn't believe him.

"Yeah, Fairbanks, Alaska," Langston smiled sweetly. One day those charming white teeth of his would become harder and harder for Chanel to say no to.

"It's kind of a long story, but you see my dad was stationed there

5five years ago," he explained. "He's retired from the Air Force now, but so far my parents have decided to stay there."

"Well, that must suck." Chanel suggested.

"What does?" Langston came back.

"Being the only black family living in Alaska."

Both of them laughed at the same time.

"It's not what you think," he said. "There are plenty of black families living on the base. It really becomes your world. In fact, my best friend, Royce, and his girlfriend who graduated with me, came down here for school too. They're also black," he laughed.

God, what a beautiful smile, Chanel thought to herself.

"Really?" she replied. "How the heck did that happen?" Chanel wondered.

"Royce and I both earned partial academic scholarships," He clarified.

"Wow! Time really does fly," Langston observed. "I better get you inside before the mosquitos start biting your pretty brown legs" he said as he scratched his forearm. Chanel blushed.

Nearly three hours had passed since they met in the lobby. The two of them were so lost in their conversation that they didn't realize they had talked well past dinner time. It didn't matter though. Hungry or not, they had found someone special and both of them knew it. Chanel was beginning to feel special too. That was something she had never felt before, and she liked it. A lot.

CHAPTER FIVE

Chanel and Langston spent a lot of nights talking by the lake. Neither of them had a car, so their courtship (as Nannie always put it) was pretty simple. Meeting for lunch or dinner in the café, or chilling in the lobby of the dormitory to watch a movie was quickly becoming their routine. They were in love and everyone on campus could see it.

Langston was a bright spot in Chanel's life. He paid attention to her, while her family ignored her. Kathy barely called to check in, and never sent Chanel any money. So, whatever Langston had, he shared with his girl. At one point, they were even washing their laundry together to save money.

During the first month of their relationship, Langston talked about how he wanted to return to Alaska after only one semester. Chanel hated those conversations, but she understood why. Langston was dealing with several things at once- like losing his scholarship, his dorm had been burglarized, and he had a nine-month-old baby girl named Jasmine in Fairbanks that he was missing. He was crazy about her.

He told Chanel about the baby when they first met. She secretly hoped he would go home for the holiday break and see the baby, but come back in the Spring to give schoo l another go. Langston's mind was set and he wasn't changing it.

"I hate this place, man," Langston said.

"Why do you hate it so much?" Chanel asked.

"Why do you love it so much?" He questioned sarcastically.

Eventually, without any pressure from Langston, Chanel began to feel like she needed to do something to change his mind about staying. Up until now, they really hadn't had any alone time. They were always interrupted by some obnoxious co-ed when they tried to cuddle on the sofa in the lobby. Chanel fixed it in her mind that if she and Langston could be completely alone, just one time, that it would make all the difference in the world.

I have to show him how much he means to me, she thought. Besides if I don't, how will he remember me? How will I stand apart from any other girl he's dated?

Chanel designated the night of USD's Homecoming game as the night she would give her virginity to Langston. They rented a hotel room downtown, just to be alone. She was scared, mostly about what Kathy would do to her if she found out. Plus, she had no clue what she was doing.

Langston insisted, "We don't have to go through with it. I'm content with being able to spend the night in the same bed, holding you."

But Chanel had her mind made up. This was the only way she could be sure he would remember her if he left. But it wasn't the mind-blowing experience she hoped it would be.

Afterwards, as she laid there next to Blair Underwood, staring up at the raggedy ceiling fan over the bed she thought, I guess we'll just have to do it a couple more times before he leaves to make sure it took.

When Thanksgiving break came around, Chanel asked Langston to join her for the three-day break at Kathy's best friend Eva's house. They had become close back at Bridgewood, but Eva and her family moved back to San Diego a couple of years before Chanel started school there. She lived a half hour from campus. Langston declined the invitation. He said he was uncomfortable at the thought of the two of them possibly having sex in a stranger's house. Chanel was uncomfortable too, but she only wanted to spend more time alone with him before he was gone for good.

The end of the semester was quickly approaching, and Langston had no plans of changing his mind. Even with him and Chanel being intimate now.

Within two weeks of the holiday break, the inevitable came. No amount of (sexual) convincing had worked. Chanel had given her most precious gift away to a man she was never going to see again. The day she had dreaded for a month and a half was staring her right in the face. The semester was over. The first-year freshman had performed exceptionally well in all of her courses, but Langston was going back to Alaska. Chanel didn't move out of the dorm when most of the other girls did. Instead, she stayed on campus as long as she could to spend more time with her first real boyfriend, but today her ride back home was leaving and she had no choice. Chanel cried like a baby all morning. She shed as many tears as someone sending their loved ones off to war. They had spent five hours together the night before, but it didn't help. Langston was the love of her life and the first man who had loved her back. The likelihood of losing him was tearing her up inside.

"Okay, Chanel you ready to roll?"

Kenya, her suite mate, was giving her a ride back home, and they were already an hour behind schedule.

Chanel's emotions were on a rollercoaster. She was losing her first love and Kathy didn't even want to make the four-hour trip to bring Chanel home for the holidays and semester break.

With tears in her eyes, Chanel shouted back to Kenya, "I'm coming." She and Langston were embracing in a corner outside in the courtyard.

"Don't cry, girl," Langston said. "We will see each other again."

"You promise?" Chanel questioned back.

Langston pulled Chanel close to him and squeezed her tight. Kissing her forehead, he said, "I promise. You'll see me sooner than you may think. Call me tonight when you get home, okay?" He looked Chanel in her teary eyes and kissed her sweetly on her pouty pink lips.

"I will call you when I get there." She replied sadly. They exchanged I love you's, then Chanel hopped into Kenya's red pickup truck and waved goodbye to her Blair Underwood.

Four hours later, she was back in Bakersfield. She hadn't been home for a visit the entire semester, but Kathy didn't seem excited to see her when she walked in. To think she had been away at school for the past four months and Kathy didn't even hug her daughter when she came in the door. JP and Kathy were living in a different apartment now. It was a small, one bedroom unit, but very nice. It was Chanel's home for the semester break.

That night, as she made a pallet on the living room floor, all she could think about was Langston. What was he doing? Was he thinking about her too? She couldn't call him because Kathy was on the telephone until 11 o'clock that night. Even though Chanel was 18 now and a sexually experienced woman, she was still too afraid to use her mother's telephone after a certain hour, especially to call a boy.

Langston would have to wait until the morning.

Instead, Chanel laid there alone wondering why Kathy was so distant. Most parents probably had welcome home celebrations and cookouts planned for their kids when they returned. Ericka hadn't even called to make sure her little sister got home okay. Chanel tried not to focus on the gamut of emotions she was feeling. They ranged from disappointment to anger then loneliness. She just wanted her family to proud of her for a change. Would it have killed them to show they were happy for me to be home?she thought o herself.

Chanel buried her wet face into her pillow so no one would hear her crying. Her first night back home was the toughest. Eventually her tears dried up and she focused on a plan to get her old job back while she was home over the next few weeks. It would be a much-needed distraction. She finally fell asleep.
First thing the next morning, she was on the phone.

"So, you want me to come in in the morning?"

Chanel was elated when her former manager offered her old job at Ralph's. She had stopped by for a visit the day after she made it home.

"Seriously?" Chanel inquired.

"Yes! We could really use your help for a few weeks while you're waiting to go back to school. So, are you coming in or not, girl?" The manager grew impatient.

"Of course," Chanel grinned as she blurted out. "I will be there at 11 just like old times." Chanel could rack up a little cash and keep her mind off Langston at the same time.

Meanwhile, she needed to get to a doctor like yesterday. She'd been very uncomfortable down below the belt for a few days now, but she was too frightened to mention it to Kathy or even Langston for that matter.

I sure hope he didn't give me anything, she thought. What if Kathy finds out? If it's not fatal, she will kill me for sure

Thankfully, she had enough sense to catch a city bus to the local charity hospital emergency room. Three hours later, the teenager had a name for her condition.

"You have a U.T.I.," the handsome Latino doctor said.

"Oh, my God," Chanel said, as she covered her mouth with both hands. "What is that?"

"Oooooh], not to worry," he said laughing. "U.T.I. is short for urinary tract infection."

Supportively patting her on the shoulder he said, "A few days of antibiotics will clear it right up. I will write you a prescription."

Chanel sighed in relief. She was not going to die. The doctor told her most U.T.I.'s in females are caused by wiping in the wrong direction after urination, not drinking enough water or from having unprotected sex with an uncircumcised partner. Chanel knew Langston was not circumcised and he was the likely perpetrator, but when Kathy asked why she needed a prescription to treat a urinary tract infection, the tissue paper wiping explanation went over quite well.

Two weeks into her semester break, Chanel got a call at home from Joe, Jr. He wanted to see his estranged half-sister. Joe's son from his first marriage was at least seven years older than her. The children were close when Joe and Kathy were married, but after they separated the relationships fell apart or never had a chance to blossom.

"How long will you be in town?" Joe, Jr. asked sincerely.

"I'll be here until the 15th," Chanel replied.

She was leery. It had been at least 10 years since she'd seen her brother. Joe, Jr. was a high school All-American running back, and he earned a full-ride scholarship to USC. He didn't have a care in the world. Chanel couldn't understand why their father had not shown her the same care when she went away to school, penniless. "Well, do you mind if we get together for a little while before you go? I would love to take you down to see papa and your cousins. It will be nice."

Junior sounded just like their father over the phone, especially when he told Chanel, "I can't help you," when she asked him for money to help pay for her college books.

"Okay," Chanel agreed, though unconvinced of the success of such a family reunion. "We can do that."

Chanel's "Paw Paw" was the man who raised Joe and his sister. Paw Paw was actually Joe's great uncle. Even though he lived in Fresno, California, Kathy didn't keep her girls connected with him, Joe's sister, or their cousins when she moved them to the west coast. Paw Paw still lived in Fresno, as a widower. His wife had passed away years ago. Seeing them could be awkward, but it was a visit long overdue.

Joe Jr. showed up bright and early the next morning. The two of them made use of the the hour and a half long trip by catching up on the last ten years of their lives. Her big brother insisted he wanted to reconnect with his family and promised to be there to back up the young student during her academic pursuits. Besides, he was familiar with the struggles of being a full-time college student away from home.

The joke was on Chanel early in the reunion process. Junior needed to make a stop before Paw Paw's house to pick up something from a friend. That friend turned out to be their father. At first Chanel didn't recognize the slightly aged Joe, Sr. He was thinner and somehow not as tall as she remembered, but still handsome. Chanel was troubled that her father didn't even recognize his daughter as he peered through the car window studying her face. The last time he'd seen her was seven years earlier, at the divorce hearing.

"Un-be-lievable," she said, shaking her head at the stranger on the other side of the glass.

Chanel refused to get out of the car to greet her father as the two Joes conversed outside. They went on and on for a while about how the kids ended up together and how long they would be in town. Every passing moment pissed Chanel off more and more. The older Joe was in town to check on his adoptive father who he called Paw Paw, too. His health was failing and he wanted to show support.

"When was the last time you've seen him?" her brother asked when he got back inside the car.

"I'm not sure," Chanel said, though knowing exactly when. "I was probably 11 or 12, but that was not cool. You should have told me you were planning to bring me to see him."

"It wasn't planned," he assured her. "I know he was probably more surprised to see you than you him." He stared in silence at a confused Chanel before continuing. " We have to get past everything that has or hasn't happened and start fresh. I want to have a relationship with all my siblings and Joe. Don't you?"

"I guess. Sort of. I don't know," She answered.

Chanel struggled with her feelings about everything at this point. Her mind was flooded with all the memories of abuse and her father leaving the family at their most vulnerable time. It was hard for her to conceptualize why Joe Jr. wanted to rebuild with a man who had deserted him, too. The two continued with the plan to visit their grandfather. It was a short one, but pleasant. He was always a kind man. Even though he wasn't Joe's birth father, Paw Paw never made the children feel any other way.

That night when Joe, Jr. dropped Chanel back home, he promised that he was going to do whatever it took to stay connected with his family. They exchanged phone numbers and talked about seeing each other when she came back in town for another visit.

Joe Jr. said, "If you need anything, anything at all, you be sure to give me a call."

It made Chanel feel good about finally having someone in her life that would have her back.

A few weeks later, she went back to school with more poise than she arrived with the semester before. At least now she knew what to expect. Chanel saved enough money working those few weeks at Ralph's to get a few frills for her and Tori's room. Who would have thought matching bed sheets would be a luxury? It was great returning to her home away from home and new friends, but life on campus would be a challenge without Langston there. They limited their phone conversations during the break after Chanel heard Langston speaking to his daughter's mother over the phone. She was there to drop the baby off for a visit with him, but Chanel didn't like the fact that Langston didn't tell her about it.

She had no room to judge. She went out twice with Dawson, her high school crush, after their phone conversation. They even exchanged mailing addresses and phone numbers at school to keep in touch, and Chanel planned to do just that.

Out of frustration of not knowing if she and Langston were going to stay together or face an inevitable break up now, Chanel had not taken his calls for weeks.

"Girl, you have to get out of this room," Tori exclaimed. "I know you miss Langston, but there are far too many good-looking men around here to help you get over him."

"Men? Name one man." Chanel challenged.

"There might be some at my cousin's place tonight. You should come!" Tori suggested.

"Tonight? And what makes you think I'm going to go to any party tonight?" Chanel questioned.

"Some guys from UC San Diego are going to be there," Tori said, trying to convince Chanel. "Doesn't your ex Emmanuel play football there?"

Chanel laughed to herself, "First of all, Emmanuel is not my ex. We were just friends. And yes, he plays ball there, but I haven't spoken to him since I left Bakersfield last summer." Chanel replied.

"Well, as fine as he is, you should pay him a friendly visit," Tori continued. "It will be fun. Plus, maybe he can help get your mind off Langston."

Tori was right. This "thing" with Langston was never going to work.

"He is living in Alaska for God's sake," Chanel reasoned. "I'm never going to see him again, and Emmanuel is fine!" she added. "Alright Tori, I'll go. Let me change."

Emmanuel did nothing to help Chanel forget about Langston that night. She went back to her room and had one last cry over the love of her life. Brian McKnight's song was even playing on the radio when the two Alana's barged in. They attempted to cheer her up by cooking red beans and rice with sausage at 2 o'clock in the morning. Just as they were going in for round two of the favored Louisiana dish, Chanel's phone rang.

"Hey baby, I'm surprised you're still awake," It was Langston calling from Fairbanks.

"Yeah, I'm up hanging out with Alana and Alana." Chanel smiled as she shooed the giggling girls out of her room.

"You know I miss you, don't you?" he smoothly asked for reassurance.

"No, I don't. Tell me how much," Chanel asked.

"I miss you so much; I'm considering coming back down and giving school another shot. I think about you all the time, Chanel. I love my daughter. I love her so much, but I can't get you off my mind." Langston sounded so sincere.

"I would love for you to come back, you know I would, but I don't want to talk about something that won't ever happen," Chanel tried to be realistic. "Let's just enjoy each other's company on the phone right now."

The two talked until one or both of them fell asleep. Chanel woke up to the sun blaring in her face and the phone recording repeating, "If you'd like to make a call, please hang up and try your call again …"

As each day went on, she realized more and more that it was time to move on.

Eventually Chanel did get help from a few fellows who were helping her get over Langston. She and her first love spoke weekly, then monthly, and soon not at all. But he wasn't the only one not keeping in touch.

Joe, Jr. had not made good on his promise to stay in touch, either. Chanel called him every day for a week, with no call back from him. She only had questions about some class offerings she thought her know about, but he must have suspected that she wanted money. And without notice, a month later he changed his phone number. Since she had no other way of contacting him, it was left up to him to call her. He never did. "Like father, like son," she resolved.

After a while, Langston was no longer a part of her daily thoughts, but he was not out of her heart. Chanel spent another summer in Atlanta. She got a job right away this time, working in a hotel with Ericka. Her and her husband had separated, and she thought moving to Atlanta would take her to the next level. The entire experience was a disaster, though. The sisters butted heads all the time. Chanel had to walk two miles to work nearly every day, even though her sister drove every time. She went back to school for her sophomore year in shape and with a new haircut.

She was in a new dormitory, with a new roommate for the fall. Chanel and Tori had words near the end of their second semester over something so petty; she didn't even remember what they argued about. So they decided not to room together anymore.
Chanel grew increasingly dependent on the friendships she established at school. To no surprise, Kathy didn't come to visit that semester or any of the remaining ones. Aunt Teddy did mail her a check for $25 once, but the family seldom called to see how she was doing. Chanel made weekend trips home with her new roommate when she could no longer bare the agony of staying

behind on a deserted campus week after week. She couldn't understand why her family was so detached. But it didn't fill her mind for too long. Now she was getting the attention she craved from someone else.

She never considered dating Chad Baker before, but things were quickly becoming serious. Chad went to high school with Chanel, but they didn't really get to know one another until college. He was always kind of egotistical in Chanel's opinion, but now that they were taking classes together, he didn't seem all that bad. Between her family issues and mixed emotions toward Langston, Chanel was easily engrossed with Chad. She craved attention from someone, and he went shy about giving her some.

Chad was taking the same Psych class as Chanel. He would always borrow her notes from the previous class when he didn't show up, which was most of the time. In return he would give Chanel a ride when she had to run errands. He was one of a handful of undergraduates with a vehicle.

"Hey, are you driving today?" Chanel asked.

"Yes, why?" he'd replied.

"Do you think you can give me a ride to Walmart? I need to pick up a few things for my room," she explained.

"That's cool, but first I need to stop at the bank,"he said.

"No problem. I have time." Chanel grinned.

It started off innocent enough. Pretty soon, those quick shopping trips and bank runs became mini dates. Chad would ask, "Have you eaten lunch?"

"Not yet, why?" she would ask pretending she didn't know he wanted to spend more time with her.

"Have you ever been to Houston's? They have great food," he explained.

"No, I've never been," she said.

"Would you like to go?" he asked.

Chanel responded, "I really can't spend any money right now."

"Oh, don't worry about it. It's my treat." Chad always liked to pretend he was a junior high roller, even then, but Chanel knew he was broke as hell.

Chad wasn't really her type at all. He wasn't anything like Langston. He wasn't tall, dark, or handsome, but he pursued her like no one else had done before and he was actually there with her. Back then, he had a small frame and was only about 5'5" tall, with a medium brown complexion, but he had a wittiness about him that Chanel grew fond of. He could always make her laugh and they had fun together, but Chanel knew Chad was going to be trouble. She just had no idea how much.

One day Chad offered her a ride to get her nails done. He waited patiently for an hour and when it was time to pay, he stepped up to the counter to cover the cost.

"I'll take care of it," he said.

"You don't have to do that." Chanel argued.

"No, no, no. It's cool. I want to, he said.

"What will your girlfriend think of you footingthe bill for my nails?" Chanel challenged him. He liked that.

"Who said I have a girlfriend?" Chad asked with a smirk in his face.

"Come on now, everyone knows you and Audrey are seeing each other on the regular. Don't front," She made sure to add.

"Well, she won't have anything to say about it because we're about to break up anyway." That was Chad's first lie, but Chanel wouldn't realize it until later.

As her new relationship with Chad was building, Chanel was planning to find her own apartment after her second year. She had roommates lined up to help share the load. She thought maybe living away from campus wouldn't feel as lonely when everyone escapes campus life to go home. Now she just needed some funds to seal the deal.

"So, mama, when are you going to be able to come pick me up?" Chanel asked as she was nearing the end of another semester. She was looking forward to going home to see her nephews and possibly make some money working at Ralph's again.

"What do you mean?" Kathy inquired. "I thought you were going to stay with Eva?"

"I never said that," Chanel corrected. "I want to come home. I want to get my job back at Ralph's and save as much money as I can for my apartment."

"Well, if you're planning to have an apartment, then you need to stay there and find a job there." Kathy said.

"I've been looking for something here for over a month. I know for sure I can get my old job back and at least have something saved for my new place," she explained.

Kathy pushed back, "It doesn't make sense to work here for two or three months and then leave. I'm telling you, you should stay and find something there. Eva won't mind."

"My own mother doesn't want me to come home?" Chanel questioned.

Kathy may have had a point about it being better to get a job where you will be living, but all Chanel heard was that her mother didn't want her around. And it was very clear.

Completely unsupported by her family and no visits home before the summer ended, she made it to her junior year. Chanel was about to face her toughest challenge yet.

CHAPTER SIX

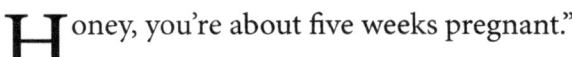

H oney, you're about five weeks pregnant."

Chanel burst into uncontrollable laughter when she heard that. The nun delivering the news assumed this information was good news, "but what she didn't know was that the laughter was completely sarcastic. Chanel couldn't believe it. Not here. Not now.

Just moments before, Chanel was studying the internal anatomy of a pregnant woman illustrated on a poster in a small room at the Pregnancy Problem Center. She had given Eva's daughter Tabitha a ride to the center and Chanel decided to take a test to kill time while she waited for Tabitha to learn her fate. There had to have been some kind of mistake.

"Tabitha is the pregnant one, not me," Chanel reasoned. "I don't feel pregnant. Aren't I supposed to feel pregnant? My period isn't even late."

The disbelief would eventually turn into extreme denial. She had two full years of school left. How was she going to care for a child? What would Kathy say? Would Chad support her? Would her friends? Chanel was not filled with joy and anticipation like most new moms. She was embarrassed and scared.

When she told Chad over the phone that day, his reaction wasn't what she expected. He convinced her he would support her and the baby, but Chanel didn't feel confident with his response. He had the keen ability to convince people of his sincerity when he was actually full of it. She hoped this wasn't one of those times.

That wouldn't be the first time Chad had said one thing but meant something else. The pattern had started early in the relationship. The signs were there right away. Chanel reflected as she sat on Ms. Eva's living room sofa.

No one likes to be lied to. There's something about dishonesty that can destroy a relationship, even before it begins. Chad had been exposed as a liar before her pregnancy, and Chanel vowed they were done many times before, though clearly they weren't. He was still dating another person when they started sleeping together. He was clever enough, even at 19, to convince her he really didn't want to be in a relationship with Audrey anymore, but he was waiting for the perfect time to break things off. According to Chad, the other young woman had done so much for him and he just couldn't find it in his heart to end the relationship abruptly.

"I feel like I owe her that much," he reasoned.

Instead, he would just cheat on her for months.

Two months into their special friendship, Chanel realized Chad had no real intention of ever informing his girlfriend about the two of them spending so much time together or breaking things off with her. So she refused to see him or take any more of his phone calls.

Not wanting to be ignored, he went as far as to tell her he did break up with his girlfriend to win Chanel back. He created a sad story about how distraught she was and how painful it was for him to watch her cry. Chanel soon discovered he had completely fabricated the story. She watched from her dorm room balcony one day as Audrey, the so-called ex-girlfriend, jumped into his car with him and drove away. Chanel gave them some time to presumably drive to his apartment and then she decided to give him a call, only he didn't answer the phone. She did.

The conversation went:

"Can I speak to Chad?"

"Who's calling?"

"Chanel."

"Chanel? Well, he's not here."

Chanel could tell by the tone in woman's voice that her instincts were right. She was the one Chad had picked up less than an hour before.

"Okay. Please let him know I called." Chanel was fuming when she hung up. "I knew it. I knew I couldn't trust his trifling ass," she fussed out loud.

Chanel's new roommate was out of town with the track team. That sucked for Chanel, especially since she had no one to vent to at the moment, nor did she have a ride to go confront Chad. She wanted to embarrass him at work.

She opted instead, to go to his place and talk to his girlfriend, convincing a friend to give her a ride over to Chad's place. When she got there, his friend wasn't at all pleased by Chanel's invasion. But she didn't care; she had to do it.

"I told you Chad's not home," the girl tried to reason when she opened the front door.

"That's fine. I will wait for him," Chanel retorted self-righteously.

Then she took a seat on the dingy brown sofa, crossed her legs and arms and exhaled furiously. Her driver took a seat next to her in disbelief of Chanel's boldness to intrude like this, but she didn't care. She was getting to the bottom of this. How could he be such a snake and lie to her face for months? What had she done to deserve such blatant disrespect? And to think, Chad wasn't even her first choice. There were men on campus much taller, sexier, and smarter, but she gave him a chance. He'd really crossed the line, plus she had really become fond of Chad, and she was hurt. Only selfish thoughts of course, not thinking his first girlfriend was there as well.

It would be an hour before Chad made it home. In the meantime, the girls went back and forth about Chad's dealings with both of them. His girlfriend refused to believe anything Chanel said. In fact, her response to everything Chanel told her was, "I'll just have to hear what Chad has to say."

Eventually he came hone to receive his unannounced surprise. As it turned out, Chad didn't have much to say. He barely opened his mouth when Chanel began her interrogation. His collective explanation for his deceitful behavior was, "I didn't want you to know."

A month after the big "confrontation," the ex-lovers were seeing each other again, but their reunion came after all the tires were slashed on his brand new, bright red BMW 3 Series Sedan.

Chad was convinced that Chanel was either the perpetrator or the organizer behind the attack on his vehicle. He believed she was the only one of the two women he'd scorned that had enough moxie to do it. He even had his goon of a friend follow her to classes and left threatening messages on her answering machine for a week afterwards.

The truth was, Chanel knew exactly who was responsible. She found out the same night his car was vandalized. What Chad didn't know is that the woman with the most nerve to trash his car was also the one that had the greatest ability not to snitch. Besides, he wouldn't believe her anyway, and Chanel didn't care.

Now, just three months after reuniting, though not as a couple in Chad's opinion, Chanel had his baby growing in her belly. They made the decision together to try to develop a real relationship this time, especially given the fact this child would forever connect them. She knew it wouldn't work, but she wanted to have a family for her baby. Chanel blamed herself this time, even though Chad made a habit of maximizing on her vulnerabilities.

Chad's reaction to the news about the baby was surprising. Chanel called him at work.

"Do you have time to talk?" she asked.

"Yeah, I'm still on my break for another 10 minutes. What's up?"

"Do you remember the other day when I told you I was taking

Tabitha to find out if she was pregnant?" Chanel spoke nervously.

"Oh yeah, that's right. Is she?" he asked

"Yep, she's almost 10 weeks," she explained

"Whaaat? What did her mama say?" Chad asked with interest.

"She hasn't told her yet. She's waiting until she can get both of her parents together first," Chanel explained.

"I know Ms. Eva is going to flip out. Tabitha's only 17." Chad laughed light heartedly.

"Yeah, well her mama's not the only mama we have to worry about." Chanel replied.

"What do you mean?" The nervousness in Chad's voice had returned.

"I took a pregnancy test too while I was there with her. I'm five weeks pregnant, Chad." Chanel cringed as the words came past her lips.

"Really?" Chad didn't seem surprised. "I knew it. I felt it."

"You felt it?" Chanel couldn't believe it. She thought for sure he would be less than enthused.
"I don't know. I kind of sensed it, I guess," he continued. "So, what do you want - a girl or boy?"

Chanel didn't know what to say. She wasn't prepared for his calmness. He didn't even ask if she wanted to go through with the pregnancy. Perhaps he does deserve the benefit of the doubt, she thought.

"A girl I guess, but it really doesn't matter." Chanel smiled in relief.

Now with Chad in her corner, Chanel's only challenge was to tell Kathy.

There was no question about how she would take the news. When Ericka got pregnant the first time, Kathy could have killed her with her bare hands. Chanel knew she had to get some things in order before she let her know. At the time, she was still living at Eva's, at least until the start of the new semester.

Now finding an apartment away from campus was no longer just a way to express her independence, it was a necessity. She couldn't exactly house an infant in a college dormitory. After she secured her own place to live, then it would be safe to tell Kathy about the baby. Until then, she spent the next couple of weeks taking pregnancy tests from the drugstore just to make sure there was really something to tell her mother. That way, Kathy would have no room to criticize her about her choices.

She had a part-time job with campus catering, but her hours weren't consistent enough. She needed a steady paycheck to care for a kid. Chanel found a regular part-time gig at the YMCA. She was hired to clean the locker rooms and restrooms with another worker, but after about three weeks, she was forced to resign. The morning sickness was kicking her butt, lasting way past morning hours. She was late nearly every day and she could hardly tolerate the fumes from the products she cleaned with. This definitely was a wrench in her plans, but jot a deal breaker.

The best news came a few days later when she found out her apartment application was approved. She couldn't be more relieved. Alana C., and Carmen managed to find someone that☐ rents to full-tim e college students. It was a cute three-bedroom townhouse. It wasn't as close to campus as she would have liked, but it was theirs, and there was nothing Kathy could say about it. Except he fact that she didn't have a car. But she knew she had to tell her.

She stressed all morning on the day she planned to tell her mother the news. Chanel rehearsed what she wanted to say for hours, but it wouldn't matter. She waited until she was alone at Eva's house to make the phone call. It was a good thing she did. Kathy's reaction to her pregnancy was painful. Chanel knew she would be disappointed, but, in some way, Chanel hoped she would at least be supportive.

"Hey mama, I'm calling to let you know we got our apartment and I want to give you my new address."

"Oh okay," Kathy replied unimpressed. "Who are you living with?"

"Do you remember Alana C. and Carmen? You talked to them both a few times when I lived in Grant Hall."

"Is Carmen the one from New Orleans? The short, brown skinned girl with glasses?" Kathy pretended to remember.

"Yes, that's the one. Her grandmother co-signed on the place for us and we got approved."

Chanel's voice and hands were shaking. This was the hardest thing she ever had to do.

"We don't have a phone number yet," she continued. "But it should be set up this weekend." Chanel was trying her best to stall, but it wasn't working. She took a deep breath and let it out.

"I also needed to let you know something else too. Last month, I…I found out… I'm pregnant," she finally blurted out.

"What! You're pregnant?" Kathy yelled.

Chanel felt all the air leave the room.

"I don't want to hear that!" her mother continued. "I can't believe you were foolish enough to get yourself in this situation, Chanel. What are you looking for from me? Approval?"

"No, ma'am," Chanel replied cautiously. "I just needed to let you know."

"Well, it doesn't have anything to do with me. It's your choice. You can have as many children as you want," the new grandmother said coldly. "I guess you'll be dropping out of school next then?"

"No, I'm not. I'm staying in school," Chanel stated matter-of-factly.

"Well, like I said that's your choice. Bye." Kathy hung up without waiting for Chanel to answer.
Chanel felt chills runs down her spine. Her sweaty palms were still trembling, partly from relief that it was over, but mostly because her mother was so callous. She didn't ask if she was getting prenatal care or if she had found a job to care for the baby, or even how she was feeling. Chanel wouldn't hear from Kathy again until she was close to delivering, six months later. It never mattered how badly

her mother treated her, she always hoped for better.

The lack of support from her family was the pits, but each day Chanel could also see Chad slipping out of her corner . Instead of visiting or checking in on her every day, she was lucky to hear from Chad once a week. She felt so abandoned. Chad lived as if nothing was changing for him. While she struggled to find health care coverage and meet prenatal and WIC appointments, he went to frat parties and wherever else he felt like. He spent more time away from the mother of his child than he did with her. He hadn't even told his family about the baby. Chanel knew he was embarrassed, not about having a baby, but about having a baby with her. She didn't have a perfect family, like he had perpetuated his own to be. Chanel's mother and father weren't financing her education or bankrolling her living expenses. She scrapped to get by. Chad couldn't appreciate that, but liked to compare Chanel to his not so ex-girlfriend, Audrey, wherever he could . Matters were only getting worse for the young mother-tobe as the days and weeks passed.

One day, it became painfully clear to Chanel that Chad was disinterested in committing solely to her and their child. It was more painful than any cold shoulder Kathy could give her. She was washing some clothes he'd left after spending a few nights at her place. The best she could figure was that Chad was just making up for lost time. He'd never done that before so she hoped Chad was turning over a new leaf. Chanel found a letter folded away in the pockets of his jeans. It was from his ex-girlfriend, the one he supposedly spared from heartache a year ago. In the letter, Audrey expressed how angry she was that Chad had abandoned her.

She wrote, "So you can just knock me up and walk away from your responsibility?" Audrey was pregnant too. Chanel couldn't believe her eyes. At that moment, Chanel's focus became less about her and Chad's future together and more about a plan for caring for her baby alone.

"There's no way he can be there for two children," she thought. "He will have to make a choice and I know where I stand."

Chanel didn't hold back when she confronted him.

"Why didn't you tell me she was pregnant?"

"I didn't tell you because there won't be a baby," Chad urged.

"What are you talking about?" Chanel demanded. "She said she's pregnant with your child."

"Yeah, but she's having an abortion. That's why I didn't tell you. What would be the point?"

Chad was one selfish son-of-a bitch. Somehow, he persuaded Audrey to get rid of her baby to save his own skin. There was no way she came to that decision alone. She loved Chad too much, but a week later, Audrey went through with the abortion just as Chad said.

Since Chanel no longer had to contend with the challenge of Chad having two mouths to feed, she started thinking strategically. In order to do that, she needed to take a break from Chad. It was nearly impossible to focus with his flaky position about being her boyfriend and a father at the same time. There was no question, she had to complete school. She had to secure her future, but it was going to be tough.

"If I quit now, I'll never finish." she reasoned.

But in the back of her mind, Chanel knew that the one thing she wanted most out of life more than anything, was to have a family of her own. Like it or not, she had started one with Chad. As horrible as it sounded, maybe the abortion was a blessing in disguise. It left the way clear for the two young parents to build a family together. Chanel never held back her feelings about the two of them working hard at staying together. Chad didn't disappoint. He did an excellent job playing emotional games with her for months. He knew Chanel was vulnerable because she wanted so much for their baby to grow up with a mother and father - not like she did.

He first led Chanel to believe he wanted to get married. Chad's idea of proposing was asking, "Would you like a new purse or an engagement ring for Christmas?"

He knew how she would respond. He would begin his sentences regarding plans for the future like, "When we get married," or, "After we get married."

When Christmas came and went with no engagement ring, Chad began to frequently ask Chanel to pay bills for him. She came to his rescue most times because she constantly felt like she needed to prove how loyal she could be.

Once he asked, "Do you think you could loan me $75 to cover my portion of the light bill?" Chad had roommates too. "I'll pay you back when I get the money from my dad," he assured her.

The problem was that Chanel had just deposited her paycheck into her account that morning, and it was only $98. She needed gas and groceries, and after all, she was pregnant. They both knew Chad

had no intention of paying her back, but she had to show him she had his back. Unfortunately, she had hoped to get love for what she did instead of for who she was to him.

"Yeah, sure," she answered hesitantly, wondering how she would eat for the next few weeks, or days, for that matter.

"Cool. Let me get my coat and you can drive me to the payment center and write the check."

Chad's propensity toward arrogance began to emerge. Chanel had always suspected, but he kept it well hidden. He had no reservations about literally taking food out of his unborn baby's mouth just to cover his own ass. Chanel was smart enough to know her situation with Chad was not going to make her happy, not even in the long run. But her baby was worth the sacrifice. That's what she reasoned in her mind. She didn't want to see her child grow up with the reality of rejection and embarrassment of not having a father. She knew first-hand what that was like.

By her seventh month of pregnancy, Chanel found out from one of Chad's roommates that he was seeing his ex-girlfriend again. That was why he kept failing to show up for those doctor's appointments he promised to go to. In actuality, Chad was rekindling his relationship with Audrey, who he claimed was now his best friend. The day of Chanel's sonogram was the worst.

"Ms. Banks, if you like we can get you in and out a little early." The nurse at the Woman's Center was so pleasant. She was an older lady, no more than five feet tall, wearing a cute set of blue and pink scrubs with balloons all over them. "Do you want to come back now and change into your gown?"

"No ma'am. I'm waiting for my boyfriend. Can we wait for my appointment time?"

"Sure. No problem. The nurse said. We'll call you back in about 10 minutes."

"Thank you," Chanel smiled. She was anxious and could feel the muscles tightening in her belly.

She thought, "Surely he will show up today." He'd missed the other appointments, but this was important. They would see their child together for the first time. He couldn't miss this.

"Ms. Banks, are you ready?" Ten minutes had gone by so quickly. Chanel gazed outside the window one last time checking for Chad.

"Yes ma'am. If someone name Chad Baker arrives, please send him back to my exam room. He's my boyfriend." Chanel hoped he would come, but she knew in her heart the chances of him showing were slim to none. Chad didn't even have a car of his own anymore.

"I sure will, Honey," the nurse responded sweetly.

Chanel's eyes began to well up with tears as she changed into the exam gown. She was so distracted she couldn't even remember whether the nurse instructed her to remove all or none of her under garments. She left them all behind in the changing room and went into the dimly lit, cold exam room across the hall.

"Are you okay?" the tech asked.

"Yes, I'm fine," Chanel lied.

"Okay, lie back on the table here and relax," the tech said with a smile.

In seconds, Chanel was looking at the most beautiful little heart pumping as strong as she had dreamed. There was her child, as healthy as a horse.

"Can you tell what it is?" Chanel inquired.

"I sure can. Would you like to know?" the tech asked.

Chanel glanced at the door hoping Chad would burst through. She paused a few more seconds and answered, "Sure, why not?"

"You're having a boy," The nurse said with excitement.

Chanel was crushed that Chad had missed out on this exciting moment. What could possibly be more important than learning the sex of your first child? Whatever or whoever it was definitely more important than she thought.

When she got home that night, she decided she would let things go with Chad.

If he doesn't want to back me up, fine, she thought.

She crawled onto her bed, laid on her back and stared at the ceiling. As the gravity of her situation weighed on her mind, a warm tear drop crept down the side of her right temple. She thought about the challenges that were in store for her and her baby boy.

"God, I need your help," she prayed. "I'm not going to be able to do this on my own."

Chanel always wanted to enroll in law school immediately after undergraduate studies, but that wouldn't be practical, at least not now. She certainly never thought she would face single motherhood. Chanel had plans for her life; she expected a good future. Her present circumstances were certainly threating those plans.

Chanel worked in the evenings and weekends throughout her pregnancy as much as she could. Chad showed up sporadically to plant seeds of hope that their baby would be raised by both parents. She realized later, it was just a strategy he was using to keep her available for him.

He shocked her one night when he showed up for her birthing class at the hospital. It was the class that teaches new parents how to change diapers and feed their newborn babies. Chanel barely recognized him when he walked in because the lights were down for the film. Chad sat down and put his arm around her shoulders, in an effort to display support, either to convince himself or the other new parents, but Chanel wasn't buying it.
He invited her over to his apartment after the class that night so the two could talk about where things were going. Shortly after they arrived there was a knock on the door. Chad looked surprised.

"Who is it?" He asked.

"Audrey," the voice outside replied. Chad appeared genuinely stunned.

He opened the door and in walked little Ms. Sunshine, herself, Chad's precious ex-girlfriend. Chanel hadn't seen her since she learned about her pregnancy and later abortion a few months before. She seemed to be in high spirits and quickly made herself comfortable on the sofa. Chanel labored to get from her comfy spot on the floor and onto her feet. Lately with her increasing size, sitting on the floor had become more suitable than a traditional chair. She headed for the exit, but Chad stopped her.

"Chanel, where are you going?"

"I'm going home." She replied. Chanel was surprised.

"We haven't finished talking," he insisted as he followed her down the stairs and into the parking lot. He assured Chanel he didn't know Audrey was stopping by and he really wanted to finish their conversation.

A protest like this from Chad was very unusual. He was always eager to abandon ship in any situation which threatened to expose him as a lying jerk.

Audrey had followed them outside and was poised to join in the discussion. She only aimed to incite matters when she butted in the conversation and asked, "Chad, how you gonna take care of a baby when you don't know if it's yours?"

"Like hell he doesn't know!" Chanel shouted. "Were you there when we were in bed together?"

"Calm down, Chanel," Chad urged. "And Audrey, chill out. I know the baby's mine and I will be there to help take care of him."

"Well, Chad all this back and forth emotional bullshit you've been putting me through ends tonight," Chanel continued, leaning against her car for support. "If you're going to try and make this work, you need to say so now. Otherwise, I will walk away."

"Look, I care about both of y'all," the liar started. "I really do, but in all honesty…" He hesitated. "I care about her more." He looked at Audrey. In response, Ms. Sunshine folded her arms and smirked at Chanel.

Chanel felt her heart sank. There she stood, carrying his baby, who was doing flips in her belly at that very moment, and his father tells her in front of the person who aborted his other child that he cares about her more.

"Well, since you care about her so much, you should keep her under control. She doesn't know anything about me or my baby. So she should keep my name and anything about my son out of her mouth." Chanel angrily waddled to the side of her car and jumped in to leave. She kept her composure until she started her engine and saw Chad and Audrey heading back upstairs.

"Why do I keep getting hurt like this?!" She shouted. Chanel put the car in reverse and drove away in tears.

Two months later, and one week before she delivered the baby, she saw Chad again. He was supposed to come by to help her move into another townhouse with her roommates. Chad showed up hours after the work was done, asking to borrow $100

Chad's idea of helping was making Chanel's bed with sheets and blankets as she settled into her new bedroom. She and her roommates agreed that the downstairs bedroom would be best for her, considering the baby was coming any day, and having to climb stairs could potentially be a problem. Their instincts were right, and so were Chanel's.

CHAPTER SEVEN

---◦---

The baby was due late February, but Chanel was convinced she would deliver on Valentine's Day. She even told anyone who asked that February 14th was her due date. That weekend, both her roommates took separate weekend trips home. Chanel pleaded for one of them to stay.

Carmen said, "Girl you ain't gone have that baby this weekend."

"I am. I'm telling you," Chanel insisted. "My doctor asked at my appointment today if I'd been having any contractions. He said it will be any day now."

"I'll be back early on Sunday anyway. You'll be fine," Carmen assured. "Just don't walk around too much."

The two of them laughed.

Chanel had no choice but to walk. She went to work catering, as scheduled the following night. Her supervisor and the entire catering crew were on pins and needles. Chanel had to advise them that medically, she was in labor. When she got through a ten-hour shift, it was midnight, Valentine's Day. Chanel went home, showered and got in bed, but couldn't sleep. She was troubled at the thought that Chad didn't return her calls from earlier when she tried to give him the update from the doctor.

He is so selfish, she thought to herself as she struggled to get comfortable.

At 2 a.m., she still hadn't fallen asleep, so she called Alana over to her place. Alana D. only lived five minutes away. It's a good thing she did because she was the only one around who cared enough to take the phone call of a pregnant woman after midnight.

"Something just isn't right, Alana." Chanel said. "I think I'm in labor."

"Well, I guess you wouldn't be joking with me at two in the morning." Alana sounded completely out of it. "I'm on my way."

When Chanel hung up the phone, she paged her doctor. By the time Alana arrived, Chanel's call was returned.

"We have to go to the hospital. My doctor said to meet him there."

"Are you in labor?" Alana questioned excited, but rubbing her red, watery eyes.

"He said since the discomfort is enough to keep me awake, I should come in."

Chanel tried calling Chad again before they left, but there was still no answer at his house. She knew where he was, but didn't have the number. Chanel was hoping his roommates would hear the voice message and contact Chad for her.

The drive to the hospital was less than 10 minutes. Chanel refused to undress after she was checked into Labor & Delivery. She had a history of overacting throughout this pregnancy and every time she made an appearance at the treatment center, she was eventually sent back home. Plus, she never really believed the baby would actually come on Valentine's Day. Still in her coat and street clothes, she questioned the nurse.

"Am I having this baby today?"

"Well, darlin', I won't know anything until have a chance to examine you. You gotta get undressed." Nurse Donna replied.

"Okay. Well, I'll just take my bottoms off. That's all you really need anyway." Chanel said smugly.

"Girl, you are a mess," Alana chimed in. "Let this woman do her job."

"No, she's fine. Just lie back on the bed., the nurse said.

Chanel cringed slightly at the sensation of the ice-cold gel lubricant covered latex exam gloves the nurse had. About 30 seconds of the discomfort had passed into the exam, and her patients were wearing thin.

"So, am I having this baby or not?" Chanel asked again.

"Hon, you are 3 centimeters dilated. You're not going anywhere," the nurse said.

Terrified, Chanel looked at Alana and said, "Okay, let's get this show on the road." Then she began to undress completely.

Alana now had the task of locating Chad and calling Kathy. She wasn't pleased with her job, but she sucked it up and tried her best.

"He's going to miss it," Chanel repeated. "I know he's going to miss it. He promised he would be here." Chanel was painfully panicked.

"Just try to relax. He'll be here," Alana tried to reassure her friend.

At that moment, the door to her room swung open. For a mere second, relief filled Chanel's heart, but it was Carmen. So her anxiety went right back up. It was early and Sunday, and she was back like she promised. But so far she was the only one keeping promises. All of a sudden, Chanel began to cry uncontrollably.

"Ooooh, Lord! I walk in the door and she has a contraction. Dammit!" Carmen was always the panicky type, but too dramatic.

"No, I'm not! Chanel shouted. Still in tears, with sweat now beaded up on her forehead she said, "You were two hours away and managed to get here. Chad hasn't even called."

Her friends tried to console her, feeding her ice chips, while rubbing her hand and back. It. Wasn't Chad, but it was a great replacement for the time being.

After another hour of increasing physical pain and progressive labor, the epidural was finally ordered. The anesthesiologist came in, bursting with energy. "We're going to have a baby!" He shouted joyfully. "I just need you to sit up as straight as you can and let your legs dangle off the side of the bed like you're sitting in a chair."

Alana helped Chanel position herself and again she began to cry.

Everything was happening so fast.

In a few short minutes, Chanel's legs and feet were growing numb. Her tears had stopped as she began to accept that Chad probably wouldn't make the delivery. Alana had to fill in when the nurse directed Chanel to start pushing.

"You stand over here and hold her hand, darling," Donna instructed. "Now we're going to count to three together, and you're gonna give me a strong push on three, okay?"

In unison the three women chanted, "One, two, Push!"

"Okay, again," Donna coached. Just then, the door to the room opened again. This time it was Chad dressed in his Sunday's best. He made it after all. He quickly changed into a pair of scrubs and took over Alana's position. He was so nervous and scared that he didn't make a peep, just got into position as he should've been already.

"Whew! What a relief!" Carmen jeered from the corner of the room. "I didn't think we were going to make it through this." She laughed nervously. Carmen had spent the past ten minutes with her head buried in her lap while Alana helped Chanel push.

"Where were you?" Chanel asked him furiously
.

"I was on my way to church," Chad responded casually.
"I've been trying to reach you all morning," Chanel wouldn't let up as if his whereabouts were more important than her labor and delivery at the moment.

"Hey, hey, Honey - you have to take a few deep breaths and relax,"

Donna said in efforts to regain control of the situation. "We're gonna try to push again."

This time Donna took position at the bottom of the bed and reached underneath the sheet.
"Okay, again. One, two, PUSH!" they all shouted together.

Nothing was happening besides more water rushing down Chanel's leg and the fetal monitor beeping angrily. Donna went to get the doctor who had not made an appearance all day.

Once he finally came, he examined the expectant mother for an entire 30 seconds and determined the baby was showing signs of distress each time Chanel would push.

"It looks like we're going to have to take you upstairs for a C-section." He ordered.

"What! A C-section? Nooo, no," Chanel cried as she did not take the suggestion of surgery very well. A caesarean birth was what she feared most throughout her pregnancy.

The unsympathetic doctor just gave the order and left the room. He didn't care what she did or didn't want.

"I can't have surgery. If I have surgery, who knows when I'll be able to go back to classes," Chanel tried to get Chad to understand. An explanation wouldn't have been necessary if he had paid more attention to her throughout the pregnancy.

"Listen, there's nothing you can do. It will be fine," Chad tried to calm her down, clearly it wasn't working.

Chanel cried all the way to the operating room. Within 10 minutes of the doctor giving the order, she was holding her sweet little baby in her arms. Weeping and wailing like most newborns, the baby boy stared back at his mother as if he were looking at an old friend. He let out a deep tiring sigh as he attempted to scan the room with one opened eye, the other shut tightly in protest.

Chad whispered to Chanel, "See, aren't you glad I was here?"

Without acknowledging Chad, she kissed her baby's tiny face and just like that, she was out like a light.

She woke up in recovery cold and shaking like crazy. She called out for someone, anyone.

"I'm freezing. I can't stop shaking." Someone gave her a blanket and she passed out again.

When she awoke again, peeking out of one eye, in much the same way as her newborn son, she scanned the room quickly. There were quite a few faces smiling back at her, but her mother Kathy wasn't one of them; neither was Chad.

"Wow, he couldn't even wait for me to wake up tomake sure I was okay?" she thought to herself.

Chanel was so embarrassed. Everyone was there except the people she believed should have been there. The story Ms. Eva told her was that Chad left minutes before to go to work. Kathy got the message from Alana, but she was going to attempt the four-hour drive down the next day.

Carmen was sweet enough to spend most of the night with her

before leaving to go home.

As she lay there in bed, alone in that cold hospital room, the new mom reflected on the day. Christopher Aiden Baker was born healthy. With the exception of the unexpected C-section, she was doing well too. That was the good news. Unfortunately, everything Chad promised about helping her take care of their son didn't seem so reassuring now. Their new son was not even 12 hours old yet and his father had already disappeared before he even knew she would wake up in the recovery room. How could Chanel have confidence in him as a father?

Four days later he did reappear to drive Chanel and little Christopher home from the hospital. She was hopeful he would step up and do the right thing, but he was out of the door before Chanel could settle in her bedroom with the baby. She had to yell out to him from the front door as he headed for the car, "Please go to the store and buy some formula so that I can feed your son". It was so sad and only getting sadder.

She knew marriage wasn't in the immediate future. They were so young, but she did wish he would commit to her for the benefit of their child. Chad just didn't get it. He didn't share the same sacrificial ideals for family as she did, but an unexpected shimmer of hope emerged from obscurity. When Chanel found out Langston, he former love, was trying to get in contact with her after a couple of years of no contact, her faith in the possibility of a family of her own was restored.

"Girl, Langston called you again," her roommate Carmen yelled from the kitchen downstairs." You need to call him back before he loses interest in your single parenting behind. Carmen could always be counted on for comedy.

"Langston?" Chanel said puzzled. Are you sure? Carmen was silent.

"What does he want?" Chanel thought out loud. "I wonder if he knows about the baby?" she directed to Carmen. Christopher was nearly three months old by then.

"Well, I sure as hell didn't tell him," Carmen responded jokingly. The two of them laughed. "Just call him back and see. He said he would be in town."

"Oh, my goodness," Chanel was somewhat suspicious. She thought she would never see him again.

All sorts of thoughts went racing through her mind. Would he be angry about her having a child with someone else? Did he want to rekindle their relationship? What could it be?

Chanel remembered two weeks before she last spoke with Langston, he confessed to her the real reason he was so adamant about returning to Alaska. He was expecting another baby. His second daughter was born a couple of months after he left school. She was crushed. Langston had lied to her their entire relationship. Cutting things off when they did seemed to be the best chance for her to heal. Now she was over it, but she still couldn't imagine why the one she never stopped loving wanted to talk to her now.
The next day he called again. This time she answered, hoping to get some answers.

"Hey, baby," Langston spoke with the same smooth tone he always had. "How have you been?"

"Baby?" she questioned in her mind. "I haven't been your baby for a while now," Chanel corrected.

"I'm sorry. You're right. How are you, Chanel?" he asked politely.

"I'm really good, just surprised to hear from you though." She responded.

"I know, but I've been thinking about you a lot lately," he said in hopes to softing her up.

"Sure, you have," she laughed.

"No, really I have. I miss you a lot," Langston said convincingly. "You know you'll always be my girl."

"Well, I'm someone else's girl now." Chanel lied.

"Yes, you are," he agreed. I heard you have a baby now."

Smiling from ear to ear she said, "Yes I do. I have a son. She paused and said, "But I'm not his father's girl anymore, either. I was just kidding with you before."

"Ooooh, okay," Langston sounded relieved. "So, do you think I will have a chance to see you tonight?" He asked. "I have to leave in the morning."
"What's the rush?" she inquired.

"I'm only passing through. I fly out to Philly in the morning," he informed her.

"Well, I don't have anyone to watch my baby right now," She replied.

"That's okay," he said. "I want to see your son. He must be adorable, just like his mother. Besides I have my daughter Alexis with me. I'm taking her to Philadelphia to see my grandmother."

Chanel was speechless for a moment. Hesitating, she finally spoke up. "Oh. Okay. Umm, well give me the address where you are, and I will stop by for little while to say hi."

"Great. I can't wait to see you." Langston sounded genuinely thrilled.

But Chanel wasn't thrilled. She hung up and called Alana on the phone for support. Alana agreed to ride over with her to see him, and Carmen agreed to stay home with Little Chris. She didn't really want to bring her young son out at night to a stranger's house. Chanel argued with herself and Alana the entire drive over. Was she ready to see the face of the little person who separated her from her first love two years before? Could she handle the feelings that were bound to come rushing back like raging waters when their eyes met?

"I can't do this," she shared with her friend.

"Girl, don't worry. You'll be fine." Alana comforted. "We'll just stay a minute."
Alana was right, she was fine. Her eyes welled with water when she laid eyes on Langston, but she contained herself nicely. He was as handsome as she remembered. He hugged her tightly and for that moment she felt very safe. He kissed her cheek as always. But reality quickly set in when she glanced down to see the sweet little brown face of his baby girl, Alexis. She was reaching upwards for her daddy to pick her up. The two-nyear-old looked up at Chanel with same dark eyes as her father.

After two hours of catching up, and Chanel gently braiding Alexis' hair, she hugged Langston and wished him well. He promised he would keep in touch. Chanel was surprised that her feelings for him had been completely resolved. There would be no reconciling for the former lovers, and Chanel was content with that certainty.

CHAPTER EIGHT

———◦◦———

When her baby was six months old, Chanel moved into a place of her own. She felt like she was burdening her roommates and she didn't want to feel that way any longer. The transition didn't go as smoothly as she would have liked, though. During the application process, Chanel found out Kathy had set up an electric bill in her name when she was still in high school. The account was in collections, so Chanel's rental application was initially denied. In disbelief, Chanel called Kathy and questioned her about it.

"Did you know there is an electric bill in my name that you never paid?" she asked.

"What are you talking about?" Kathy wondered.

"My credit report is showing an outstanding bill for Dominion Power Company. It went into collections four years ago. It can't be mine because I was in high school," she explained

"Oh yeah," Kathy remembered. "That's right. I forgot all about that."

"Well, the apartment manager is denying my application until it gets paid."

"Well, how much is the bill?" Kathy asked.

A highly-agitated Chanel replied, "It's $180."

"Hmm," Kathy thought of a good response in her favor. "Just pay it and I'll give you the money back."

"I really don't have any extra money, Mama, because I have to pay my deposit, too," Chanel explained.

"I will send the money this week, Chanel," Kathy insisted.

In the end, Chanel ended up paying the debt. She had no other choice. She and Chris had already been kicked out of a friend's apartment by their grandmother. Chanel and the baby had been staying over until she found a place of her own. It didn't take long, but the mean grandmother claimed she was becoming irritated whenever Christopher cried. They were forced to move out immediately with only a day's notice.

A week later, Chanel went to pick up her belongings that Chad was storing at his place until she was ready to move. It was the least he could do. The day she went, she brought Carmen along to wait in her truck with Christopher, while Chanel went to the door to see if someone was home. She went expecting to be disappointed as usual.

She knocked a few times, but there was no response. As she walked away, heading to the truck, her attention was drawn above her head. She saw Chad's roommate Jeremy standing on their balcony with Audrey. Apparently, she and Chad were seeing each other again. Somewhat puzzled about being ignored, Chanel addressed the roommate.

"Jeremy, didn't you hear me knocking at the door?"

"Look, I don't want to get involved," he replied.

"Involved? Listen, I just stopped by to pick up my stuff," She said with a blatant attitude.

"I will let Chad know you came by, but…"

Chanel interrupted him, "Do you have a problem?" she questioned Audrey.

"No, I don't have a problem," Audrey responded with attitude.

"Then why are you staring at me?" Chanel could feel the blood boiling in her veins.

"I can look at who and where ever I want, □" Audrey clarified.

"Well, why don't you come down here so you can get a better look?" Chanel sarcastically suggested.

"I don't have to come anywhere," Audrey replied back.

Fine, Chanel thought. Out loud she said, "Ok, I will just come up there then."
She headed back up the steps of the garden style apartment. Chanel was fed up and all she saw was red. Chanel's pregnancy had stopped her from laying into this woman like she wanted, but now…. well, now she wasn't pregnant.

Jeremy was brave enough to open the front door this time, probably in an effort to hold Chanel off, but within moments the three of them were engaged in a brawl, and there was no turning back. Jeremy made a great attempt to disengage the match. He was sandwiched between the women when Chanel reached over his shoulders, grabbed Audrey's hair and slammed her head against the door frame. His second attempt to overpower Chanel was equally unsuccessful. He struggled to back Chanel away from the steps.

He yelled, "Chanel, stop it! Please! We're going to fall!"

Chanel unrelenting shouted back, "If we fall, we fall!"

In that instance, she really didn't care how things ended. She had suppressed so much anger and frustration. Chanel couldn't hold back now that it was finally coming out. Besides, Audrey had it coming. She was finally going to pay for all the horrible things she said and the lies she spread about Chanel and her baby. Chanel landed a few more jabs before forcing Audrey and Jeremy back into the apartment doorway with a strong kick. The front door slammed shut. Chanel was locked out.

Sweating and nearly winded, she stormed back to the car. Carmen and Christopher were patiently waiting, completely unaware of the drama that had just ensued.

"Girl, why are you sweating?" her baffled friend asked. "Where is your stuff?"

"You won't believe what just happened. I just had a fight," She explained as she panted.

"What? With who?" Carmen's eyes grew wide.

Chanel explained as they drove home.

Late that evening, Chad showed up at Chanel's new place pounding on the door. She opened the door and he stormed in.

"I don't even care about the fight," he started. "I just want to know why you said what you said."

Still in a heavy-eyed haze, Chanel remembered that during the altercation she conveniently revealed to Audrey that Chad wasn't as devoted to her as he liked people to think.

Yawning and rubbing her eyes she answered back, "Well she needed to be knocked down from that high horse she seems to be riding on all of the time."

She continued, "And if you were being honest with her, there wouldn't be anything for me to tell.

Chad couldn't argue with that. He eventually calmed down and spent the night on her living room sofa. He was apparently still more concerned about Audrey than Chanel and their family he lied about wanting so many times in the past.

Chad moved in with Audrey two months after the altercation. Chanel realized she couldn't put her life on hold any longer. She had given Chad enough time to make the choice to live with his family or without it. He chose the latter.
So, she followed his lead and started to see other people. She had landed a life-saving job that summer which helped stabilize her financially, at least for a while. There was a guy she met in her training class that she was kind of interested in. He also attended USD, but the two of them had never met before. After a few weeks of training for work and hanging out for lunch, Chanel suggested they get together after work one day.

"Awww! Okay," he said. "You're serious?"

"Yes. I am. Why not?" Chanel responded.

"That would be cool. We can do that," he said blushing.

"Well, are you busy this Saturday? I would like to see The Best Man. It's showing now, I think," she suggested.

"Yes, I think you're right. Okay. It's a date, □" he confirmed.

But it wasn't really a date - at least not a date for the two of them. The guy picked Chanel up from the baby sitter's house, but said he needed to swing by his apartment first to pick up something. When they got there, he invited Chanel to come in and have a seat. While she waited, his roommate appeared and introduced himself. Seconds later, there was a knock on the door. It was another young woman, whom Chanel assumed was the guest of her date's roommate. The two of them jumped in the car. When they bought the movie tickets Chanel found out the woman was actually her date's ex-girlfriend, and his roommate that tagged along was apparently her date. This was unusual and made her a little uncomfortable and second guess her decision.

She reasoned to herself, Maybe seeing other people isn't the best thing right now.

Chanel needed to work on a plan to finish school and be able to support herself and Chris at the same time. She was spared the humiliation of having to see the date from hell again day in and day out at work, but at a cost. After their training class ended, the company divided the trainees into two groups. One group was selected to start their full-time assignments on the morning shift, and the other group was given evenings. Chanel was assigned mornings. The problem was that she would have to quit school in order to work morning hours. In a class full of college students, none of the former trainees were willing to make the switch with her. Chanel had promised herself no matter what, she would finish school. So she was forced to quit the job.

Working a full-time job while also a full-time student was beyond difficult. In the year after her son was born, Chanel worked as a telemarketer, a caterer, a customer service representative, and a cashier to make ends meet. It became unmanageable to pay someone to watch Chris in the evenings on top of the regular hours of day care.

Of course, Chad didn't make things any easier. It was nearly impossible for the two young parents to communicate. Every time Chanel called his house to speak with him, she would answer and make Chanel explain her reason for needing to speak with Chad. Audrey was constantly threatened and her insecurities were always showing.

By the next day, the phone number would be changed. This cycle repeated at least three times, which is the number of times Chanel called the lovebirds' nest. Chanel despised their relationship. She hated it so much because Chad allowed Audrey to dictate how involved he was or wasn't in his child's life.

Without an open line to communicate, Chanel found herself becoming a stereotypical baby's mother. She had to make appearances at Chad's job just to talk to him about Christopher's needs. At first, he wasn't paying child support, so Chanel sometimes resorted to non-conventional ways of acquiring cash. Sometimes she had to clean the apartment of a friend for 20 bucks every other week, just to keep diapers for the baby. At her lowest point, Chanel was donating plasma at a donation clinic. She could go there on a weekly basis and make $35. It was good for gas money and groceries, but it did nothing for her self-image. The clinic was in the seediest part of town and often reeked of urine and cigarette smoke. Most of the other donators were homeless or worse off than she. But even this clinic played its part more than Chad.

The father of her child stood by like a spectator on the sideline, still enjoying college life, going out to parties with friends and staying out all night. Chad never had to miss one party or even a class because of his responsibility to Chris, since he and others around him convinced him that he had none.

Disconnection notices and threats of eviction came every month. Chad had agreed to deposit his portion of daycare in her bank account once a month and help buy formula and pampers here and there. He didn't follow through, and the final straw was when two of her daycare check payments bounced. The daycare director advised Chanel of the baby's fate one day at pickup.

"Hi there, Ms. Banks." The director stopped Chanel as she walked in. "Can I talk with you in my office, please, before you pick up the baby?"

Chanel already knew why she wanted to talk. She'd been avoiding the woman for weeks.

"Sure," she hesitantly replied.

"I'm sorry to be the bearer of bad news, but you're now two payments behind on Christopher's tuition. Unfortunately, if you don't pay the balance in full by the end of this week, we're going to have to remove him from the roll," She said with concern.

"I understand, but I'm only one behind now," Chanel contended.

"No actually, it's two," the woman corrected. "Remember you pay one week in advance, so you need two payments to be on track."

Chanel was furious on the inside. The very next morning, she missed classes to make a trip downtown. She went to the District Attorney's office to file for child support. It was a day she sincerely hoped would never come. Chad had everything he needed, why didn't Christopher? Of course, Chad wasn't happy with her decision and he didn't visit their son or have a kind word to say to her for weeks after he was served. But it was worth the possibility of her child being financially taken care of.

The court date came just a few days shy of Chris' first birthday. It was humiliating to stand before a court full of strangers and share details of one's personal life. What's worse is that Chad hadn't even tried to explain his failure. It's probably because he knew it wouldn't have made a difference. Chanel's mind was set and he didn't have a leg to stand on. Maybe his handicap is why he brought Audrey to the hearing with him for support.

"Will the parties in the matter of the State versus Chad Baker please step forward?" the clerk opened.

Chanel reasoned in her heart that Chad had not followed through on his commitment so she needed to do what was necessary to gain support for their son. Chad's public defender was, however, fixated on why Chanel wasn't working outside the home to support the baby.

The state's attorney quickly fired back, "Judge, the child in this matter is well below the age of five- school age. As such, the mother's employment status is not a matter requiring any further discussion."

In ten minutes, the judge ordered Chad to pay $165 per month. Chad worked part time and attended school full time, so Chanel could not expect much more than that. Collecting the child support would be another battle altogether.

"I just don't understand why you felt it necessary to bring these people into our lives," he said.

"Well, I gave you a chance, Chad, and you failed. I've told you a hundred times, my priority is to Chris. I could care less if you like me or not," Chanel explained with all seriousness.

Chad knew Chanel was right. But instead of adopting her decision to put their son first, he took the approach of making Chanel regret ever exposing him in this way. He cut out his weekly visits to see the baby and came one a month instead. Four months after the child support was ordered, Chanel had not received a single payment. Chad thought he would teach her a lesson and make her wait for the payment instead of helping her in the meantime. Chad was not happy about the order, as could be expected. Even though his payments were not to start for another month and a half, he refused to give any assistance in the meantime. Of course, get was hurting his child more than Chanel.

CHAPTER NINE

———◦◦———

Chanel was under so much stress trying to finish up school. Graduation day couldn't get there soon enough. She had failed most of her classes the previous semester when she gave birth, and had to repeat those courses during the summer session in order to graduate. Little Chris was in a new daycare and a seasonal job as a census worker was monumental in getting her through that last semester. She was hired as an enumerator and was assigned to canvass her own neighborhood, which didn't require a car. It's a good thing, since she was already bumming rides to school.

After successfully hiding her car from the bank for nearly six months, Chanel's car was eventually taken after she threw a rod in the engine and couldn't drive the vehicle to a secure hiding spot. Her field job as a Census Enumerator allowed her to work on the same street she lived on, so she only needed to get a ride campus for classes.

Not having a car complicated matters even more, so graduating was nothing short of a miracle. That's why Chanel didn't take kindly to most of her family choosing not to come down to share in this historic occasion. She was, after all, the first in the family to go to, and finish, college. Joe had turned down his invitation and so did her maternal grandparents. Joe's adoptive mother died not long after he and Kathy were married and her adoptive grandfather had finally succumbed to his many health issues. In the end, Kathy came with Aunt Teddy. Teddy was retired from the Marines now and Chanel was just happy to see her there for support, even if she did bring her lady friend Dolly or Daphne.

A very pregnant Ericka skipped out on attending the big event, too. She delivered another little boy two weeks later, her third child. She married her second husband a month after moving back to Bakersfield from Atlanta, and from Dallas the second time. Chris and Chanel went home for a short visit to meet the baby.

The day after Chanel returned to San Diego, she received some disturbing news.

"Hey, what are you guys doing?" Kathy asked over the phone.

"Oh, we're not up to much. I just came in from test driving a car. I think I might buy it." Chanel had received enough money from a settlement to pay cash for a used car. Chanel and her family were members of a class action lawsuit that her mother and Aunt Juanita found out about several years before. They signed themselves and their children up for the suit when it was reported that an oil and gas company back home in Texas was on the hook for knowingly exposing thousands of residents living in a small area near its chemical plant to harmful fumes over an 18 month period. The chemical not only spilled into the air, but was also traced in the drinking water causing some serious health problems years later for some people living there. Kathy and her girls had lived in the area temporarily with Juanita while attempting to escape abuse at the hands of her ex-husband.

"Okay. Well, good. Make sure you have a mechanic to take a look at it though," her mother advised.

"So, what's going on?" Chanel was very curious. Kathy didn't usually call unless something was up.

"Well, I called to give you some sad news." Kathy paused. "Little Tyson died this morning."

"What?! What are you talking about?" Chanel couldn't believe what she was hearing. Tyson was Ericka's newborn baby. She had just held him in her arms less than a week ago.

"Ericka called 911 for a paramedic this morning because she said he wasn't breathing and uh…. when they got there, he was already dead,"

"Oh, my God. That is just crazy!" Chanel repeated. "It just doesn't make sense. What was wrong with him? Was he sick?"

"Well, they're going to do an autopsy, but the doctors think it was crib death. Who knows, child?" Kathy let out a loud sigh. "We'll just have to wait and see."

Chanel wanted to call Ericka, but she couldn't bring herself to do it. She thought there had to be more to the story. She blamed her.

It's her fault, she thought. I know it is.

She and Chris went back for the funeral a week later. Much of their family from out of town came for support as well. Their grandmother, Nannie, was there, their cousin Robi, Aunt Juanita, Tiffany and Aunt Teddy too. Chanel barely spoke two words to Ericka while they were there. She preferred instead to watch Ericka. She wanted to see if there were genuine signs of grief, or if she was putting on. Chanel wasn't really able to judge one way or the other, but Ericka's actions at the wake certainly were bizarre.

After the crowd of mourners faded away and many had left the chapel for the lobby, Chanel became curious of the whereabouts of her big sister. She didn't have to go far to find her. She found Ericka in the chapel sitting on a pew, but she wasn't alone. Ericka had taken Tyson's body from the casket and there she sat cradling him as if she were putting him to sleep. Both Jeremiah and Andrew, her older sons, were each sitting on both sides of her. Appalled, Chanel didn't know whether to scream in horror or take the deceased infant from her arms and put him back in the casket herself.

Instead she fled back to the lobby to find Kathy.

"Mama, you are not going to believe this!" she spoke in disbelief even after witnessing it with her own eyes. "Ericka is in the chapel holding the baby."

"What baby?" Nannie questioned intently, overhearing the conversation.

"Tyson. She took him out of the casket!" Chanel informed.

"What? Is she crazy?" Kathy questioned in dismay as she and Nannie rushed back to the chapel.

Nannie sat on the pew next to Ericka and put her arm around her for comfort. Kathy on the other hand took on a more direct approach. "Ericka, what are you doing? Do you know how crazy you look right now?" she yelled.

Ericka, completely unfazed by her mother's judgmental tone, continued to rock her dead child in her arms.

Kathy, more unyielding now, spoke loudly, "Well, are you planning to go down in the ground with him too?"

As insensitive as it was, that was the jolt Ericka needed. She began sobbing as Nannie, took the baby from her and placed him back in his casket. Ericka and her two other little boys stood over the coffin and said their last goodbyes to the infant. Chanel shook her head in dismay as she walked away, still shocked by what had just happened. Everyone got through the rest of the day without any other weird stuff happening.

Back in San Diego, Chanel's landlord eventually followed through on their threats to evict her. She had exhausted every program she could that would provide rental assistance, food, or help with utility payments. Chanel had no real plan, only ideas of moving to a new city for a fresh start. So when her friend Temi, who she had known since freshman year in college suggested they go to Washington, DC together and live as roommates until they could support themselves independently, it sounded crazy.

"It will be good for both of us," Temi said. "Besides, what do we have to lose?"

"You're right, girl," Chanel agreed, "but it's so expensive out there. I've never even visited the east coast." The only images Chanel had of DC were ones she'd seen on television. Temi, on the other hand, had spent many summers and holidays in the area visiting family and friends.

"Think about it Chanel," Temi insisted. "You said yourself, you weren't ready to apply to law school," she conveniently reminded her worried friend. "DC would be perfect for a government major to gain valuable work experience. Plus, all of our expenses will be cut in half as roommates."

Temi had a point, Chanel thought. "Let's do it," she confirmed.

Chanel went full force applying for jobs in the nation's capital. Her first interview was with the Federal Elections Commission. It was over the phone, but they showed a lot of interest. The way she figured, law school was on hold, but she had a degree in political science and that could at least get her through the doors of a lot of government agencies. Even without a job in sight, Chanel gave away or sold everything she had and started the mental journey to the Promised Land. For five months after the eviction, she and the baby slept on the couches or living room floors of friends in San Diego, with occasional visits to family in Bakersfield and Atlanta, when she could scrap together $100 for airfare. Those visits were actually cries for help, but no one listened. That wasn't the kind of life Chris deserved.

At one point, Temi proposed that Chanel and Chris come to New York to visit her and her new boyfriend. She had gone there after graduation. It sounded like fun to Chanel. She'd never been there before, and she wouldn't have to worry about being a burden to anyone, at least for a little while.

"Okay, girl," she said to Temi over the phone. "I got a cheap flight on AirTran and Chris flies for free. We will be there the day after tomorrow."
"Awww, I'm so excited!" Temi squealed. "You're going to love it here. We will pick you up from baggage claim at the airport. See you soon."

It was just what Chanel needed to get her mind off things. Christopher was extra cranky on the flight over, but the change of scenery made it all worthwhile. It was the middle of winter and freezing cold. Chanel had never really seen snow. It was like a different world.

"It's amazing here. There's so much to see and do, not like at home," Chanel commented to Temi.

"I know, right?" Temi agreed as she picked up Chris and carried him outside. Her boyfriend, Shay, was waiting in the car.

"Babe, this is Chanel and little Christopher," she introduced them. "Say hi, Chrissy." Christopher waved his chunky little hand.

"Hi, it's nice to meet you both," Shay said.

"Good to meet you too, finally, and thanks for letting us come up for a visit." Chanel smiled.

"It's no problem at all. We're happy to have you here."

The couple was happy to have them there. Chanel and Chris spent the next few weeks relaxing and enjoying their new-found piece of mind. Chanel got a grand tour of New York City for the first time. They took the ferry into the city almost every day just to hang out, and they even saw parts of New Jersey when visiting Shay's friends. It wasn't a beach vacation, but it was something new and different. Chanel appreciated it while it lasted. But of course, it was still a non-working vacation.

Reality set in as her funds got lower and lower. She'd been drawing unemployment this whole time, but she was now weeks away from it ending. In addition to receiving Chanel's mail at her place, Alana was also kind enough to deposit the checks into Chanel's bank account. She knew she had to get back home soon and resume preparing for her and Chris' future. So after a little more fun, she did just that.

They flew back to California after nearly a three week stay, and immediately drove up to Bakersfield to see Kathy. It was during this trying period that Chanel saw Joe for the last time. Chanel and Chris went with Kathy nto a small grocery store to get some things for dinner. As the three of them walked along the isles, Chanel heard a man's voice ask,

"How are you doing?"

Without a second thought Chanel ignored the voice, dismissing it as some guy trying to make a pass at her. When the question was asked again by the strange voice, Chanel turned around to make sure her toddler sized baby boy was keeping up behind her. In one glance of the stranger, she knew it was her long-lost father. When he reached out to pick up his grandson, Chanel grabbed the baby first and headed straight for the exit without even acknowledging Joe. Kathy stayed behind to chat with him and finish up her shopping.

Chanel sat in the car seething. How could he? How could Joe think for a second it was okay for him to touch her son when he clearly hasn't wanted anything to do with her for years. And what was he doing here anyway?"

Joe never tried to contact Chanel after that or any other time. Kathy tried eagerly to make her daughter feel guilty about her actions, but Chanel wouldn't budge. After all, she should be upset with him too.

Chanel became more determined than ever to make a better life for her and her son, but the plan to move to DC with Temi was almost shot to hell. Temi had decided to stay permanently in New York instead with her boyfriend. So, Chanel had to make a radical decision. Sleeping on sofas and feeling like a burden every where they went was not working. The night she and her two- year-old spent the night in her car was a breaking point. The baby slept while she kept watch for hours in an empty parking lot. The scene served as the final straw.

The idea of taking Chris thousands of miles from his family, including Chad was not a pleasant thought. He left Audrey once again and moved into a single-family home with some friends from work. She brought the baby over for what would be his last visit before she moved. It had been a few weeks since he and Chad had laid eyes on each other. Chanel offered Chad one final opportunity to prove he would support her efforts to do what was best for the baby.

That night, she told Chad she was seriously debating moving to DC to raise Chris alone, or staying in town so they could parent together.

"I really don't know what I want to do, but I'm not happy," she shared. "What do you think about having Chris spend his nights here with you? I'll pick him up during the day, but I'll have peace of mind knowing he's sleeping in the same bed at night - at least until I figure out what I'm going to do next."
"Naaawww," he replied. "That's not going to work."

"It's not going to work?" Chanel didn't understand.

"It's not going to work because I never know when I might have company."

Chanel could hardly befriend what she was hearing. This was selfish, even for Chad. How could he be so self-centered? Here his son is, without a place to lie his head at night and his only excuse for not being willing to keep him is that he can't predict when he'll have company over?

Chanel needed no further convincing that moving away was the right thing to do, with or without Temi.

Chanel thought, This is his son, not a pet that needed a sitter, but his own flesh and blood. Chad didn't care one way or the other about her or their son. It was a painful reality. Hed been showing her since she was pregnant, but now get was telling her in so many words.

She drove away in tears over what he said. She was so upset, she needed to pull over to get herself together.
 Eddie, a mutual friend of hers and Chad's, saw her crying in the parking lot of the gas station.

"Chanel, what's going on?" he asked from the window of his car. "Are you alright?"

"Hey, Eddie... um, I really need sosomeplace to stay tonight – me...me and the baby." Chanel felt so vulnerable. "Do you mind if we come over?"
"Not at all," he said. "What's going on?"

"I'll tell you about it when we get to your house," Chanel replied.

"Okay. Just follow me home, okay?"

Christopher had fallen asleep in his car seat by the time they arrived. She gathered some of their belongings for the right and went inside.Chanel cradled him in her arms as she sat down on the cold, red leather sofa at Eddie's townhouse. She immediately released her frustrations in a much-needed vent.

"I can't believe Chad would bug out like this." Eddie had confidence in his old friend.

"I wouldn't have believed it either if I had not heard it for myself," Chanel countered.

"I just don't get it. I really don't get it." Eddie shook this head. "Maybe you misunderstood him or he misunderstood you."

"What other way was I supposed to interpret it, Eddie? He said Chris couldn't stay there!"

"I guess you're right," Eddie finally agreed. "That's so messed up, though. Anyway, you two can stay here for as long as you need to. My roommate won't be back for weeks. He's not taking classes this semester."

Chanel was relieved as she drifted off to sleep on the cold, red sofa. She could finally sleep comfortably without worry.

The next morning, she took her car in for an oil change. She made a quick stop by Alana's to pick up the final unemployment check she was expecting. It hadn't come, but her tax refund was there.

"It's a good thing I came by," she said to Alana. "I've been waiting for this."

Chanel cashed the check and grabbed dinner. She and Chris

spent what would be their last night in Eddie's apartment, and in California.

The next day she knocked on Eddie's bedroom door and told him she and the baby were leaving.

"Okay," her unsuspecting friend said. "Do you want me to leave the key under the mat for you?"

"No, I don't need the key. We're not coming back tonight," she replied.

"Are you staying someplace else tonight then?" he questioned. Eddie looked genuinely concerned.

"Nope. We're going to DC, " she explained.

"When?" Eddie was stunned.

"Right now." Chanel said.
"What do you mean right now? How?!" he exclaimed.

"I'm taking my baby in my car and driving there right now." She was unflinching and it felt great.

"Are you crazy? Maybe you should think about it." Eddie tried to convince her to stay, to reconsider, but it was of no use.

"I appreciate you for helping us out. I really do, but this is what I have to do. I can't stay here anymore." Chanel carried Christopher to the front door and walked out. Eddie followed them, stumbling with sleep still in his eyes.

"I don't mind you staying here if that's the reason you're leaving. You really can stay until you figure things out." Eddie watched as Chanel buckled her son into his car seat.

"I have figured things out, Eddie," she replied. "I know I can't stay. We'll be fine. Trust me." She kissed her friend on the cheek and got into her car.

Eddie could tell by the look in her eyes there was no amount of convincing that would get Chanel to change her mind. It was made up.

"Well, call me if you need anything," he relented, "anything at all, okay?" Eddie said, with a troubled look on his face.

"I will." Chanel said as she drove off with little Christopher waving good bye to her friend.

Eddie was the only person she said good-bye to. Kathy wasn't aware of her plans, and neither was Chad. She had not even discussed leaving with Alana the day before. Up until the day before she didn't know she was leaving.

"I guess I'll call them when I get there - wherever 'there' is," she thought.

CHAPTER TEN

The morning Chanel left San Diego was like any other one. Everything she owned was in the car. She and the baby had been driving around with all their earthly possessions for months, so there was no need to pack. When she said good bye to her friend, Chanel was filled with so much uncertainty, but with a heart full of hope. That day had become the single moment in her life where she felt most helpless and had no other choice. Now she had to surrender her will andher life into the hands of God. He was all she had at this point.

They stopped in Tucson, Arizona the first night. By day two, she was in Abilene, Texas. She and Chris stayed there with her grandma Nannie's baby sister. It had been years since she'd slept on Texas soil.

Chanel was exhausted. The morning came rather abruptly. She barely slept. After a huge breakfast and a few hours of small talk, Chanel and her son were back on the road, but not before getting hugs and kisses to last a lifetime from their great aunt. This wasn't something she was use to, but she always wanted it.

The day's plan was to cover four states before taking a rest. But traveling with a toddler was a challenge. If Chanel could drive one hour without the baby wanting to climb out of his car seat to get his hands on a juice or other snack, she'd be lucky.

"As long as mommy keeps those chubby little hands full of Cheetos you'll be alright, huh honey bunny?" she joked with Chris.

The toddler smiled back like he knew what she meant. He wasn't saying too many intelligible words then, but that didn't stop him from trying to sing along to Destiny Child's "Survivor" playing repeatedly on the car radio.

The most difficult leg of the journey came as she prepared to cross the Georgia state line. It was day four. They reached a turning point while traveling north on I-59 in Alabama. There was literally a fork in the road where Chanel had to decide to continue north towards Chattanooga, Tennessee or east towards Atlanta. Atlanta represented a safety net. Chanel knew Aunt Teddy was there and she could have a reasonably good start - maybe not the one she wanted, but a good one, nonetheless.

Those 45 seconds felt like hours as she processed all the pros and cons. In disbelief, with sweaty palms wrapped tightly around the steering wheel, she veered left, forever altering the course of her life.

A few hours later they arrived in Knoxville, where they spent the night. She filled up her gas tank for what felt like the hundreth time, picked up chicken nuggets from Wendy's for her hungry little companion, and rented a room at the Knights Inn.

She put the baby down for the night and began to pray in the cold, dark room. Chanel started thanking God for her life and for Him taking care of her and Christopher throughout their journey. Within seconds of opening her mouth, Chanel was in tears.

She asked, "God, what I'm I doing? I'm not equipped for this. I have no money, no real plan, and no one is on the other end of this journey, waiting for us. What am I going to do?" Chanel was sure she heard the voice of God. With her head, and heart, bowed in reverence, she heard Him. In that moment, in the stillness of time, as she sobbed, she heard her Father's voice.

He said, "Go. I will take care of you. Trust me."

Her tears stopped. How could one sign bring so much peace in the midst of so much mental turmoil? Chanel continued the journey with no source of income. She would finish it on God's grace - that much, she knew. God would have to have some major tricks up his sleeves to pull this one off, but Chanel had never been surer of anything in her life.

Chanel picked herself up off the floor, wiped her nose and face, and went to sleep.

The first sight of Washington DC was frightening. They entered from Virginia Route 66. The cars parallel parked along the roads made the lanes so narrow. M Street was a nightmare; Cyclists and pedestrians were dodging out into the middle of the street, giving no thought to the cars nearly mowing them over, not to mention huge city buses lunging out in front of moving traffic without a signal. Everything was moving extra fast and there was still fresh snow on the ground. All the excitement drove Chanel to tears. Christopher was crying too - only his tears were for something else.

"Mommy, I eat,"was the toddler's way of saying he was hungry.

"I know honey bunny," she replied. Chanel tried comforting him by holding his little fingers, which were stained with orange Cheetos cheese, with her right hand, while gripping the steering wheel nervously with her left.

"Mommy will stop real soon and get you something to eat, okay?"

"K" he whimpered back.

It was another hour before they stopped. Chanel had deemed the directions to a shelter in Virginia absolutely useless. Upon arrival at another shelter, the building was completely locked down. It was a Sunday, but she thought, People need help on the weekends, don't they?

When she saw a sign for Motel 6 from the highway, the exhausted traveler immediately pulled over. She bought one personal pan pizza and rented a room for the night. Chanel was relieved to have a few hours to regroup, but her focus was soon interrupted when she turned on the shower to bathe and a disgusting pink liquid sputtered out. They had to be moved to a different room and it took another half hour to get Chris settled again. Things did not look very encouraging, but little did Chanel know that night would be the last night she and her son ever had to worry about where they slept again.

The next day was Monday, and Chanel immediately went to the telephone book to find a local shelter that would take them in. Check out time was 11:00 a.m., so she didn't have any time to spare. She was turned down by what seemed like every emergency shelter in the area because she was not a resident of the state or because they were over capacity. She grew worried as she looked into the eyes of her son. Christopher had no clue his future was in jeopardy as he hopped up and down on the motel bed. Finally, someone had mercy. She was referred by an angel in Virginia to a battered women's shelter in the District.

The sweet voice on the phone said, "Honey, if they don't have room for you call me back, and we will make room. There's no way I'm gone leave you and that baby out there like that."

It was the same shelter that was closed when she showed up the day before. She was overcome with emotion and crying uncontrollably when she made the next call. Chanel struggled to communicate to the woman on the other end how desperate her situation was.

Shaken and hysterical, she blurted out, "My baby is only two years old, and we have no place to go. I'm from California and I don't know anyone here."

"Calm down, sweetheart. Calm down," the woman said. "Where are you now?"

"I'm in a motel room," Chanel answered wiping the tears from her eyes.

"Okay, but what city are you in?" the woman tried to reason.

"Oh, I don't know. I just stopped at the first motel sign I saw." Chanel was trembling by now.

"Alright," the woman said, "We will figure it out. I want you to hang up the phone, call the front desk and ask where they are located. Then I want you to call me right back. You got it?"

"Yes, ma'am. I got it," Chanel replied.

She hung up the phone and dialed '1' to speak with the front desk. She discovered they were in Capital Heights, Maryland, a place Chanel had never heard of. When she called the shelter back, the woman gave her step by step directions to their address. Thankfully the instructions were accurate since Chanel didn't have fuel to waste. She gassed up with her last five bucks.

She pulled into the drive way of My Sister's Place, a huge orange and brown house situated in the heart of Washington, DC. It was located on a heavily-traveled main artery, which pumped thousands of commuters throughout the city every day. The house was four levels, bigger than any home she had ever been inside of. There were seven women living there with their children at that time. She and Chris were given their own furnished room, and they shared one hall bathroom with another family.

That first night in the shelter was surprisingly one of the most peaceful nights of her life. Chanel slept like she didn't have a care in the world. She had her assurance from God that from that point on, all their needs would always be taken care of.

Over the following few days, she hit the ground running every morning. She had no problem complying with the requirements of staying in the shelter house. All the registrations and medical evaluations were met without resistance from Chanel, and she was ready to find work. She had to support herself, and living in a shelter was not the life she wanted long term, or even short term. The decisions and moves she made now would determine how long she and her baby would be living there.

In only six weeks, Chanel had landed a job, and Chris was enrolled in daycare just blocks away.

The job was as an administrative assistant at a female residential facility. The executive director of My Sister's Place had a contact there and had arranged for the interview. The facility housed women in recovery from alcohol and substance abuse. It was new territory for Chanel. She had never spent any significant time around anyone with mental health issues or addictions, among other problems, but she was eager to find stability again. So, she happily did the job!

On her first day, exactly what those other problems were, were eloquently laid out for her. Sister Mary, the program director, was delighted she'd taken the position and whisked Chanel away into her office as soon as she walked into the door.

"We are so happy to have you here," the nun said. "But, I want you to understand that the women who live here have a number of issues outside of homelessness—most of them have struggled with drug and alcohol dependency most of their lives. There are some ladies here who've been diagnosed with bipolar disorder, paranoia, or schizophrenia, which they are under a doctor's care for. A few others have HIV/AIDS and some of them have criminal records and delinquencies of some sort."

Chanel folded her hands and smiled apprehensively and wondered to herself, How did a sweet little nun end up in such a place?

Sister Mary continued, "Now, part of your responsibilities will be to help me and the other staff keep the women on schedule, appointments with doctors, drug counselors, probation officers, and with completing their chores. Do you think you can handle that?"
Heck no, Chanel thought to herself. I didn't sign up for this drama. I thought I would just be answering phones and typing letters. You want me to be a social worker too? But she smiled sweetly and said, "Sure, that won't be a problem at all."

It felt good to earn a paycheck after so long without one, even if it meant an occasional run in with a chemically dependent, homeless, sociopathic women. With all the craziness was worth being able to provide for her and Chris.

The facility had a strict rule that the only calls the women could take on the front office lines were those from their doctors, probation officers, attorneys, or others that were somehow aiding them on their road to self-sufficiency. In one instance Chanel pissed off one of the residents so badly, she actually feared the woman would physically assault her.

The woman's name was Toni. She was 45 years old and had a history of heroin addiction. She was HIV positive, with a negative attitude. She lived in the facility years before, and walked around with a chip on her shoulder because she was back now. Chanel was constantly reminding Toni she could not use the office phone to make personal calls to her friends and family. One day, Toni insisted Chanel let her know when her daughter called for her. But Chanel followed all of the rules and didn't want to jeapordize her employment.

"She will have to call you downstairs on the pay phone," Chanel sternly insisted.

"I told you I'm not waiting downstairs for a damn pay phone when she can just call up here and you let me know," Toni replied with much attitude.
"You know the rules, Toni," Chanel reminded her. "Besides, I am not your secretary and it's not my job to take personal calls for residents. So, if you want to talk to your daughter, she will have to call you on the pay phone downstairs."

Toni's tone was now really calm, but her words were anything but. "Listen to me you little bitch. When my daughter calls, you come and get me so I can speak to her."

"You listen to me bitch," Chanel replied. "You cannot use the office phone for personal calls."

"You will call me when she's on the phone or I will kick your ass," Toni threatened.

"Well, I guess we will have to wait and see." Chanel had more boldness than she thought. After all, Toni was one of the women there with an extensive police record and she probably could kick her ass. But Toni had threatened a staff member, another act which was frowned upon. Toni was evicted before lunch that day, and Chanel never saw her again.

Chanel learned a lot about life working at the women's facility. Three of the residents died in the first year, many relapsed, and some lost custody of their kids, but others fared well and were reunited with their children after securing permanent housing. Mostly, Chanel learned life isn't always fair. Each person has their own individual struggles. She also discovered how to spot an addict in the event she encountered one, a talent proven invaluable in the years ahead.

Fulfilling the requirements of her own residential program came with a reward Chanel never could have anticipated. Because of her success, she was given the opportunity to move out of the house with the other women into a small transitional apartment which was leased by the shelter. It seemed as if all of her hard work, faith and hope was paying off.

"You will be responsible for your phone bill and groceries. My Sister's Place will cover the utilities," Arnita advised. She was the Program Director. "You can live here rent free until you receive your voucher from the Housing Authority."

"No rent?" Chanel questioned. "You mean it's free?"

"Yes, rent is free, but you're still expected to save money as if you're paying rent for your own place. At least ten percent of your earnings must be turned in to us, and it will be kept in an escrow account for when you're ready to move," Arnita said.

Chanel liked the sound of that. It was just the boost she needed, the kind of break she'd been hoping for most of her life.

The transitional apartment was just that—transitional. In a few short months, they were living in their own apartment. Because of the voucher program, Chanel could reasonably afford rent on her own in the city. It was a miracle that anyone could afford to live there without it. Luckily, she was covered.

"Three years," she reasoned. "I will give this town three years' minimum before I think of going back home."

Chanel preferred to keep her communication with Chad and her family as minimal as possible. She didn't want to risk the chance of becoming homesick. Plus, she needed to maintain her sanity. At first, everyone judged her for leaving the way she did, with no job and no place to live, but she had to do it. No one realized the depth of the depression Chanel was experiencing in California. And seemingly, no one cared that much. After giving birth to Christopher, she felt more alone in the world than she ever had. No one saw her. No one understood her emotional instability. If she had not left when she did, Chanel was sure her life would have ended prematurely, and at her own hands.

She made the decision to not speak to Kathy or Chad very often. It was two weeks before she called and let anyone know they were now in DC. She feared their judgment. But eventually, people came to respect her decision, even Kathy, but Chad only grew increasingly resentful of it.

It proved to be a risk worth taking, though. For the first time in his young life, Christopher was living in a stable, secure situation, and Chanel owed it all to God. Every day she reflected on the audible promise she heard back in the motel room. Chanel's daily confession became, "God will take care of us," and her daily focus was not to be evicted again, and rebuilding her relationship with Christ. The Lord was keeping His promise to her, but she had to trust Him as she was instructed. Chanel wanted to do things right from this point on. So she focused on herself, her son and God.

As expected, the only people she knew in town were ladies she met while living in the shelter. Every Sunday, Chanel and Chris went from one church to the next on their recommendations. She drove to every corner of the metropolitan area for the Word and even when she found it, Chanel didn't feel quite at home in any of them. For months, the main road Chanel was familiar with was Rhode Island Avenue, where the shelter was located. Most days she passed a church on that street, where parked cars lined the road when they were having services. Strangely enough though, none of the women from the shelter ever suggested she attend one of those services. One Sunday, Chanel and Chris went on their own just to check it out.

There has to be something good going on in there, she thought.

There's way too many cars parked on this street for nonsense otherwise.

Chanel looked on in admiration as the pastor, who only stood only about 5 feet 2 inches, with a round face as genuine as a silver dollar, captivated the congregation with a sermon called Integrity. She was enthralled, along with everyone else, but she was more than just captivated. Chanel was home. For the first time since she left Bridgewood for college years before, Chanel knew she was exactly where she was supposed to be.

She joined The New Life Church a month later. Going forward, her life consisted of work, church, work, and more church, which was just what Chanel needed. But even with all of the religious zeal and consecration, she couldn't help but notice the tall, handsome, well-dressed minister at her newfound place of worship.

His name was Minister Kyle Anthony, but he preferred to be called Minister Kyle. He was beautiful, and Chanel wanted him, badly. She developed a genuine affection for him before they met, which was at a church concert one year after joining the ministry. She approached a man she didn't know, who didn't know her, and introduced herself.

"Hi there. How are you tonight?" she asked smiling nervously.

"I'm awesome. How are you?" the minister replied, gazing at the young woman as if he was trying to remember if he'd met her before.

Chanel could feel her knees getting weak and her palms starting to sweat as he shook her hand.

"Have we met before?" he inquired.

"No, we've never met, but I wanted to introduce myself." Chanel could hardly believe that the sentences she was forming in her head were actually coming out of her mouth.

"I'm Chanel Banks. What's your name?" She asked.

"Kyle Anthony," he spoke so eloquently. "It's very nice to meet you, Chanel."

"It's nice to meet you too. I just thought I would come over and say hello. We do attend the same church, after all," she followed.

"Well, that's wonderful," he smiled. "I'm looking forward to seeing you again then."

"Same here," she smiled back and walked away.

That was all she could take. Barely able to keep her composure, Chanel broke out in a sweat as she returned to her seat. Her heart was racing and her palms were drenched. But the sense of excitement was worth it all.

"I can't believe I just did that!" she spoke out loud to herself. Fanning her face with a Martin Luther King, Jr. church fan she said, "I must be crazy or really desperate."

The man was an anomaly to her. She couldn't just let him get away. Chanel had never seen a Christian man with a combination of good looks, charm, and talent that was not over 40 and married with children. It was like God had sent him straight from heaven just for her, and she was ready to move on with her romantic life.

The single mother definitely had more of an incentive to move on since she'd found out some hurtful news. Disappointingly, Chad had plans to marry his girlfriend and go on without Chanel and their child in his life. She had left that door wide open in case he ever decided that being a family was in the best interest of Chris. It was really dissatisfying when he chose otherwise. Equally disappointing was that Chad didn't tell her about his upcoming nuptials, a mutual friend from high school did.

By now, Chanel and rejection were old friends, but she didn't hate it any less. Even though she was not in love with the father of her child, she was willing to put the needs of their son ahead of her own personal happiness. Chad never appreciated the extremes she was willing to go through just to save their family. But the time had come for Chanel to give up and fight for her own happiness. She fought for it hard and simultaneously tryied to build something special and pure with Minister Kyle.

He was a perfect gentleman, and she thought Kyle was perfect for her. They dated a couple of months and he charmed her every time, but it slowly became clear that he didn't want the same things that Chanel wanted. As she learned, he had been married and was now divorced. He wasn't interested in making another permanent commitment to someone only for it come to an abrupt end. Chanel had to respect him for that. They remained friends, spoke occasionally and exchanged cute glances across the sanctuary from time to time. Chanel was disgusted, though. For all of her waiting, the minister was supposed to be her Mr. Thank-God-he-finally-came, a real father for Chris.

A little while after the newsflash, Chanel questioned Chad over the phone about his intentions to marry Audrey.

"So, tell me about your wedding plans," chanel inquired.

"What do you mean?" He asked, puzzled that Chanel was aware of his life changing decision.

"Have you set a date? If so, I need to know in advance if you want Chris to be there."

"Well, that's irrelevant to what we're talking about right now," he replied.

Chanel assumed it remained irrelevant. He never did fill her in on his wedding details, but two weeks before the big day, she got a call from his sister. She was upset, claiming Chad was not ready to get married. After that, it was Chad's turn to be upset and he called Chanel.

"So, are you going to let my son be in my wedding or not?" He asked.

"You must be crazy," Chanel responded back.

"Well, I'm about to buy his plane ticket and I need to know now." Chad spoke with his usual egotistical tone.

"There is no way I'm putting my four-year-old on a plane alone." Chanel shouted. "I asked you months ago about your plans and you told me then my questions were irrelevant. So, I'm sorry, but we have long passed the period of cooperation and negotiation." Chad went ahead with his ceremony as planned without Christopher being a part of it.

CHAPTER ELEVEN

It was only a matter of time before a career stint in the human services arena wore out its welcome. Chanel worked two years at the residential facility in DC before starting a new career as a legal assistant with a law firm. It takes a special individual to commit to the challenges associated with mental health and sobriety issues. After a lot of time dedicated and all of her patience gone, she realized she didn't have that special talent. But law, well, law was right up her alley.

She didn't have any legal experience to qualify her for a position as a legal assistant, but her interest in law and willingness to learn came beaming through during her interview with the firm's principal partner, Brad. So, he took a chance on her.

"So, are you thinking about going to law school?" Brad asked.

"At some point, yes," Chanel eagerly replied. "I thought this would be a great opportunity to gain some experience before going, though."

"When are you thinking about going?" He stared at her unashamedly with his icy blue eyes.

"Maybe in a couple of years?" Chanel lied. She knew full well she would be there right now if she had not received a rejection letter just a couple months before.

As an alternative, she took this job that would be more challenging than rewarding. The practice represented clients in personal injury and worker's' compensation cases. Most people are turned off by personal injury lawyers, deeming them as immoral and predatory, but this firm was different. It helped to shape a professional standard the young career woman would perpetuate into just about every arena of her life. There was structure and a standard of care present that the average P.I. attorneys advertising on television just didn't possess. As a matter of fact, Bradley and Brown didn't advertise at all. All of their clients came by referrals. Chanel respected that business decision.

However, for all the competence and skill there, there was one problem. Brad was psychotic. Law was his profession on the outside, but on the inside, there was a rock star dying to get out. He always bragged about how he once recorded an album with a band in college, and he was hell bent on reliving those glory days in the here and now.

By the summer of her first year with the company, Brad was on a rampage. He forced out his partner Alan Brown, who was the kindest and only reasonable half of the partnership. Brad even made it impossible for the tenants renting office space within the suite to stay. He converted an empty tenant space into make shift studio rooms, fully equipped with sound systems, keyboards, and microphones. He hired a crew of teenage rejects from the high school across the street to set up the rooms and tune up the equipment. The band held practice sessions in the middle of the day, all while the office staff attempted to advise clients on the status of their cases. It was ridiculous.

"Do I hear drums in the background?" the client on the phone asked.

"Uhhh, no ma'am," Chanel lied. "Maintenance has been doing work on the building all day and our office is right in the line of fire."

"Wow, it sounds like music," the woman laughed.

"Yes, it's pretty annoying. I can give you a call back in the morning and we can discuss your treatment a little further then." Chanel hurried to get the client off the phone.

The entire office was a revolving door, but no position was more experimental than the receptionist. Most times, Chanel didn't bother to learn the name of the person greeting visitors and answering phones because one was never around long enough to develop a relationship with. Apparently, they weren't the only ones planning an escape.

When Brad heard that Chanel was considering leaving the firm, he invited her to his office one evening to talk about it.

"I heard that you're in the market for a new job?" he asked.

"Yes, that's correct," she agreed.

"Why are you doing this? Are you trying to hurt me?" the control freak questioned.

"Brad, this really has nothing to do with you. I just realize that personal injury law is not the right area of law for me, nor is this office. So, if I find something more suitable for myself and my son,

I'm going to take it."

The man leaped dramatically from his chair and walked over to the ceiling-to-floor length windows in his corner office. He raised the blinds in all four windows. Looking out of one of them, he placed his hands on his hips in a very theatrical fashion and said, "Don't you realize we're about the take over this town?"

Chanel chuckled to herself, reminded of The World is Mine speech in a scene from the movie New Jack City. She took a deep sigh and rolled her eyes to keep from laughing out loud.

"I'm working on something special here," Brad continued, "And I want you to be a part of it. What can I do to get you to stay?"

"Nothing," she simply replied.

"What if I added an additional $5,000 to your salary?"

Chanel said, "Brad [thinking Nino Brown], you can add whatever you like to my salary and it would be appreciated, but it won't change my mind."

"I really want you to stay here," Brad assured her. "So, look forward to a little extra in your paycheck."

"Well, call me Gee Money," Chanel said out loud when she got her next paycheck.

On the home front, it turned out Chad's family was right about him not being ready for marriage. Just months after he sealed the deal, he started sharing with Chanel the second thoughts he was having about his decision. The only surprise was that he kept quiet about it as long as he did. It was just as well. Chanel was furious that he went through with that sham of a marriage without his only child there, but she tried her best to encourage him to work hard to live with the decision he'd made because that was the right thing to do. Chad was looking for her to agree that he had made a poor choice, but she wouldn't give him that satisfaction.

In spite of her anger, Chanel suggested Chad fly up and get Chris so he could spend Christmas holiday with his family. Chanel wasn't about to let Chad go about his life without Chris in it. That's exactly what Audrey would want.

"It will be good for you both to spend some time together," she offered over the phone.

"Yeah, I would like that, and my parents will be thrilled to see him." Chad agreed.

Little Chris got sick the morning he was leaving. Poor thing was so nervous about leaving his mother to be with the father he barely remembered. They met Chad and his new bride at the airport. Such a waste of funds for the couple, but Audrey clearly couldn't bear the thought of her precious husband being in town for a few hours alone with the mother of his child.

It was the longest 10 days of her life. Chanel missed her baby. Plus, she worried that Chad wasn't capable of caring for Chris as well as she does. But knowing Chad's parents were present did bring some sense of relief. At least Chanel knew evil Audrey couldn't kill her son in his sleep and get away with it. Based on her failure to try to bond with Christopher before the wedding, it was clear she wanted Chad to herself. Chanel eventually realized Audrey's concerns about Chad were well-founded.

After Chris' visit, Chad began to make unexpected visits to Washington, completely disrupting Chanel's life. She wasn't seriously involved with anyone by then, but she was dating. On one occasion, Chad came to town unannounced and surprised Chanel at her house. Even after flying hundreds of miles to see her, Chanel had no problem directing Chad back to his vehicle because she was entertaining male company.

"You have a serious problem, Chad. You are not free to show up at my door step unannounced and expect me to accommodate you," she said.

Chad was not pleased, but neither was her guest. Chad slept in his rental car that night.

"Serves him right," Chanel said, self-assured.

From that point on, Chad made his intentions clear. He realized where he wanted to be was with Chanel and their son. He was leaving his wife and now he wanted to be a family. To prove it to her, he cleared his future visits with her first.

It took a little time to get use to the idea of Chad being back in their lives in a real way. She was over the idea of wanting him, but she had a goal that never truly faded.

The first time they slept together, Chanel threw up afterwards. She was disgusted with herself. Before long they returned to their old patterns, patterns she had spent the previous three years breaking. No one knew what was going on between them except Alana, but it was hard for Chanel to look herself in the mirror when Chad left to go back home.

They wasted a lot of time playing tit for tat, reinventing their love for, or obsession with, one another. While Chad was convinced he was the cat's meow, Chanel doggedly tried to convince him she and Chris deserved his affection. He owned up to his mistakes, admitting he should have been there for the two of them and that he pushed Chanel to make the move across country in the first place. He promised he would do right by her and the baby from now on. Chad was planning a divorce. Chanel knew her passion was not for him, but for a chance of making her family complete for their child. She saw her father Joe walk away from his kids forever, and she was determined not to let that same thing happen to Christopher. She didn't see how the method she chose was destroying her from the inside out.

Back at work, drama was steadily unfolding. The serial micromanager tried to control everything, even how his employees celebrated holidays. For New Year's Eve, Brad invited everyone at the office to his house for a party. Not surprisingly, no one in the office was interested in attending, so they all either declined or didn't RSVP at all. The day before the merriments, he came into the office and made an announcement:

"I've invited you all to my home for a small party this Friday. Many of you have indicated that you won't be attending, but I want you all to know - if you chose not to attend, you won't be paid for the remaining hours of the work day."

The party was scheduled for 3 p.m. on a Friday. He was planning to close down the office for the party, and everyone was forced to head to his place or not be paid. Three years in, Chanel had had enough. She was so fed up with Brad's antics and the office turnover because of it. By then, she was handling the workload of three people on her own. It had all become too much, it wasn't worth the extra something on her paycheck anymore. Clients in physical and emotional pain were difficult to manage. So she resigned.

The day she was set to leave, Brad tried to convince her to stay, offering more money, and of course, more perks.

"You give me a number, any number, and I will write you a check right now." Brad nervously pulled out his check book and rocked back and forth in his chair.

"You tell me how much I'm worth to you," Chanel fired back.

"I don't know," he replied. "I can't put a dollar amount on the stress you experience in your body when you're working here because I can't feel it. You have to tell me that."

"Okay, Brad. Write me a check for $5,000 and I will stay until I find another job." Chanel wasn't crazy. She knew he would never go for it, but if Brad wanted to play games, she would too.

Brad put down his pen and said, "I'm not going to be able to do that."

Chanel walked out of his office that day knowing she had no employment prospects any place else. Her savings would only get her and Chris through two months, which thankfully turned out to be more than she needed. Luckily, she started another job one month after resigning.

Whew… God is good, she thought

Chanel wasn't free and clear of Brad's drama that easily, though.

Two months after settling into her new job, she received a Notice of Intent to File Suit, delivered to her doorstep by messenger. Brad was just that crazy—crazy enough to sue someone because his ego had been bruised.

When Alan, his old partner, left a year before, the two got into an ugly tug of war over which clients Brad and Alan would retain, respectfully. Later on, through their court battle, Alan found out about some future plans Brad had to sell his share of the practice and go into the music business full time. The thought of it was even more ridiculous than it sounded. This development was shared with Chanel and she chose to forewarn a fellow single mother still working with Brad.

"Hola Alma, it's Chanel." Alma was a native of Colombia and she'd always appreciated it when Chanel attempted to speak to her in her native tongue.

"Ey, Hola Chanel. Como esta?"

"Muy bien, Alma. Very good. Listen, Alma I have some important information to share with you," Chanel started.

"Oh, my goodness Chanel. Is everything ok?" Alma spoke anxiously with a thick Spanish accent.

"I'm okay, but you need to know about something I heard Brad is planning to do. I can't say who told me, but just know it's coming from a reliable source. He is trying to sell his practice in the next couple of months and he will let his staff go," Chanel reported.

"What? Are you serious?" Alma questioned hysterically.

"I am very serious, Alma. I wanted you to know because you're raising a daughter alone. Now that you have a heads-up, maybe you'll have some time to find something else before he goes through with it," she said.

"Oh, my gosh, Chanel, thank you so much for letting me know. This is awful. Gracias, mi amiga," Alma said with relief.

Regrettably for Chanel, the woman she helped decided to show her appreciation by bringing what she learned to Brad's attention. Obviously, he quickly denied it. But now he intended to file suit against Chanel for malice and slander. He even took his claim a little further by also accusing her of extortion. He was attempting to pass off his last offer of employment to Chanel as her effort to extort thousands of dollars from him.

What the hell? Chanel could hardly believe what she was reading. This is wild, even for a nut like Brad, She thought.

"Should I even respond to this mess?" She questioned Alan. He was the only legal professional she trusted.

"Just go ahead and write a short reply, mainly acknowledging your receipt. By not responding, you could send the implication that some of it, if not all of it, is true, in the event he's absurd enough to go through with it," Alan explained.

Chanel took his advice and wrote an answer to Brad. In so many words, she let him know his presentation of the events leading up to her leaving his firm was completely distorted, but she appreciated him for informing her of his intentions. Over the next few months, she waited to be served with a lawsuit, but Brad didn't follow through. He did, however, follow through with selling his practice and dismissing his staff, including Alma, right before Christmas.

These weren't the only crazy things going on, more family issues were peaking too. Chanel thought it would be a nice surprise to fly home and for Christopher to spend Easter with his cousins. By now, Ericka had two more children, her third son James, and a baby girl named Christina. A lot of time had passed, and the idea of seeing her nephews and niece made Chanel feel good.

"Chrissy, are you excited to see your cousins?" she asked her son. You will get to dye eggs and go on an Easter egg hunt!"

"Yeaahh" the six-year-old cheered. "When will we get there?"

The two were waiting in passenger loading and unloading for Kathy. Surprisingly, she seemed happy to pick them up when they called the day before on the phone.

"We'll be there as soon as Grandma Kathy gets here to pick us up, baby," Chanel assured the anxious little one.

Just then, Kathy pulled up in a brand new metallic gray Mercedes.

"Wow!" Chanel spoke out loud, very impressed. "When did you get this?"

"What? You like it?" Kathy smiled from the driver's seat. "Hey, Christopher. How are you?"
"Yes, it's really nice!" Chanel shouted as she loaded their luggage into the trunk.

"It's my birthday gift from JP," Kathy said as she pulled down her sunglasses from the top of her head and drove toward the airport exit.

Taking in the new car scent, Chanel immediately asked about Ericka and the kids.

"So, what are they up to?"

"I don't know, child," Kathy said. "You know Ericka's not speaking to me. I haven't heard from them or seen the kids in weeks."

"Well, she is just going to have to get over whatever she's going through because I did not fly all the way here not to see my nephews and niece," Chanel said.

"Well, you can call her and go pick them up, but don't tell her I asked to see them," Kathy explained.

Kathy and Ericka's relationship had been strained for years and there was no sign of things between them getting any better. The irony was the two didn't realize how much they were alike. Their mother was detached from all her girls, but even in that detachment, Chanel recognized Kathy stuck her neck out more for Ericka than she did for her other two children. One would think she would be grateful for that.

When they made it to Kathy and JP's house, Chanel was pleasantly surprised to see all the improvements they'd made. It had been years since the fire, and even though the remodeling was progressing slowly, it was progressing nonetheless. This time it actually felt like a home again. The garage had been converted into a large family room and they added a sunroom right off the formal living area.

"Doesn't it look good?" Kathy agreed.

"Things really look nice. JP has really done a great job," Chanel complimented. "Well, let me know if you need anything from the store. I'm about to head out to get the eggs and dye so the kids can have an Easter egg hunt after church on Sunday."

Kathy replied, "No, I don't need anything."

"So, what are you cooking for dinner Sunday?" Chanel questioned.

"Dinner? What do you mean?" Kathy looked sarcastically puzzled.

"Yes, Sunday, for Easter dinner," She reassured her she heard correctly.

"Oh no, honey, I'm not cooking," Kathy responded.

Disappointed, Chanel retorted, "What do you mean you're not cooking? It's Easter. You have to cook something, or barbeque."

"I am tired. I plan to relax the whole day. The kids can come over or whatever, but I'm not cooking anything," Kathy said firmly.

Chanel couldn't believe it. She can't be serious, she thought.

"How are you going to let us fly all the way home and not even make a home cooked meal for your grandson?" Chanel blurted out. "I told you, I'm tired," her mother insisted.

"Look, I will buy all of the food and help you cook," Chanel tried hard to negotiate, but to no avail. Kathy's mind was made up.

"I'm not cooking and that's that," Kathy ended the conversation.

At this point, Chanel was furious. She called to Christopher from the family room. "Chris?"

His big brown eyes were glued to Sponge Bob on the giant 60-inch TV.

"Let's go see your cousins," she yelled.

Ericka was more than willing to oblige Chanel's request to bring the kids to Kathy's house.

"So, when are you bringing them back?" Ericka inquired.

"It will be some time after church on Sunday. By the way, I will probably need a ride back to the airport. Do you think you can take us on Tuesday?" She asked hoping her mother would say yes and understand why. If Chanel had flown directly into Bakersfield, the flight would have cost significantly more. So instead, they flew into LAX, an hour and a half away.

"Yes, I have to go through there next week anyway. Just remind me when you drop the kids back off," she surprisingly agreed to.

"Ok, thanks," Chanel was grateful.
Hmm, she sure seems to be in a good mood, Chanel thought to herself.
Kathy was serious about not preparing any dinner for Easter Sunday. When Chanel and the children came home from church Kathy wasn't even home. So, she set the kids up at a table in the empty kitchen to dye the eggs.

"Okay guys, once we get our clothes changed and the eggs dyed we will have an Easter Egg Hunt in the backyard." At least the kids were excited about spending time together.

Standing at the sink to get water to boil the eggs, Chanel could see Kathy pull up in the driveway in her brand-new Mercedes. The shock was seeing Ericka following behind their mother in her car.

"Happy Easter everybody!" Ericka said as she walked through the door. "I brought pizza since y'all's grandmother is not cooking for us" The children were thrilled.

"If you want to cook, you go to your house and cook for your children," Kathy snapped back at Ericka.

She put two to-go bags from Grandy's Restaurant on the kitchen counter.

"What's that?" Chanel asked.

"I told you I wasn't cooking. I went and picked up something to eat for me and my husband." Kathy answered smugly.

Um, Chanel thought. "I guess I'm going to head over to wish my grandparents a Happy Easter. I'm sure Nannie cooked something. I will be back in a little while."

"Aren't you bringing the kids with you?" Ericka asked assumingly. "Well, I'm bringing Chris to see his great-grandparents."

"Why aren't you taking all of the kids?" she questioned.

"I will take Jeremiah and Andrew," Chanel offered. "But I'm not taking the little ones."

"Well, if you won't take them all, you can't take any of them," Erika said with a serious attitude.

"That's fine with me," Chanel answered. "Come on Christopher, let's go."

"Where are we going, Mommy?" the little one asked.

"We're going to see Nannie and Pop Pop. Then we'll come back for the Easter egg hunt, okay?" she assured him.

"Okay," Christopher was happy to go as long as he knew he would be back to play with his cousins.

The drive over took less than 20 minutes. Chanel slowly got out of the car and walked up the driveway to the front porch. She thought it was a little strange that her grandparents' car wasn't in the driveway, but she assumed it was her grandfather who was out. After knocking and ringing the doorbell several times, it was conclusive that no one was home.

"I don't even believe this. Where could they be?" Chanel questioned rhetorically. "I told them I would come by after church."

She walked back to the car and fished out her cell phone from the bottom of her purse.
"Mama, have you heard from Nannie or Pop Pop? Did they call you?" She asked in frustration.

Kathy, obviously enjoying her take out meal, smacked her lips into the phone, "No, they haven't called me. Why?"

"Well, we're sitting in the car in front of the house because no one is home. They knew we were coming over." Chanel was upset.

"Child, they are probably down at the casino. You know how they are." Kathy seemed unfazed.

"That is so messed up. I thought I would at least get some Easter treats while we were over here," she said sadly.

"You might as well come back over here because they are likely to be downtown all night long. By the way, what did you say to Ericka?" Kathy asked.

"What do you mean?" Chanel asked.

"Well, she stormed out of here with the kids right after you left. She said you can find your own ride to the airport."

"I should have known," Chanel said "She was being too nice. She's just pissed I didn't bring all of her children over here with me and Chris. Anyway, I'm going to wait a few more minutes for them and if they don't show up we will be on our way back to your house."

Chanel tossed the phone over into the passenger seat and looked at her little boy still strapped in his seatbelt in the backseat. "I knew we shouldn't have come home."

She spent the next couple of days trying to secure a ride back to the airport. She even called Chad's sister, who was in town visiting friends. In the end, they had to take a greyhound bus and cab to LA to catch their flight.

"This is not my home anymore," she told herself as she sat and watched her baby sleeping in a cold, hard chair in the empty airport. "When a girl comes home, she's supposed to feel like she is taken care of. She's supposed to feel safe. No one looked out for us here. No one took care of us. It will be a long time before I even think of coming back here again."

CHAPTER TWELVE

———————◦◦———————

It was a long time before Chanel fully recovered mentally. She continued a relationship with Chad for a year and a half into his marriage. She had never been more ashamed in her life. This relationship was truly wearing her out. It became difficult for her to ask God for anything now because she knew she didn't deserve His kindness, His mercy, or His blessings. She was embarrassed to go to church. She felt like such a hypocrite, but she had to go, even if she was living a life contrary to her convictions. Even though the encounters with Chad were minimal, it didn't matter. Chanel had completely compromised her relationship with God for a man, and it wouldn't be the last time.

By the end of the affair, Chad's interest and affection for her began to wane. Though they were long distance lovers, but Chanel hoped they were working towards something better for her son's sake and secretly her own too. Chanel was persuaded that moving closer was the best chance of them making their new relationship work after his divorce. Chad and his family had campaigned for years for Chanel to join them all in San Francisco so that they would be closer to Chris. His family made a strong argument that he desperately wanted to be a more present father to Christopher. Chanel sometimes even felt guilty about taking him so far away in the first place. They had been apart long enough and she was hopeful about reuniting them, even if Chad and her didn't work out.

It's a good thing she made peace with it because that relationship wasn't working.

One night she called him to discuss where their relationship was really headed. Instead of a speaking with him, she got a return text from another woman. It was obvious from her response Chanel wasn't the only woman Chad was cheating on his wife with, and the woman's goal was clearly to let Chanel know that she and Chad were together.

"I'm looking forward to meeting you," she wrote back to Chanel.

Chanel was taken aback. Finding out he was seeing someone else wasn't a complete shock because that was the way he usually operated, always booking ahead. So she expected it. The problem was that she had compromised everything she believed in in hopes of building a family, and he let her. He knew if they didn't have Christopher, there would be no way Chanel would compromise her faith or her values for someone like him. He was making a mockery of her.

As luck would have it, she had already made commitments to relocate to San Francisco, where Chad and his family had migrated to years before. A month before the move, she quit her job in DC and signed an apartment lease in San Francisco. This decision to leave was final, regardless of what would happen between them, but Chanel had to know what she would be walking into. Things were becoming more complicated. Couple or not, she thought his lies about being a family fan where separate and apart from his love for their child.

Chanel moved across the country again, but this time, she went kicking and screaming. Chad's divorce was final. He didn't lie about that part, but now his mistress, turned "love of his life" was pregnant.

She was six months pregnant when Chad broke the news to her. Chanel had come down for a week to finalize business with her move. After spending what seemed like a pleasant holiday with Chad and his family, he ruined it by telling Chanel he needed to discuss some concerns he'd been having. The first few minutes of their meeting were simple and filled with superficial talk about expectations of one another as co-parents once the relocation was final.

"Is that it?" Chanel questioned.

"No. Actually, I also wanted to let you know something else, too. I'm expecting a baby," Chad said casually.

Chanel felt her heart sink. It was a shock to her, but then again, it wasn't. She had sensed it from the moment his new woman made a declaration, just a few months ago.

In their exchange of text messages months ago, the woman delared to Chanel that she and Chad were seriously involved and she couldn't wait to meet me and get to know Christopher. In fact her exact words were, "I have every intention of being a part of Chad and Christopher's life". This stranger seemed to want to include Chanel in her plans because the mystery woman eventually started emailing & calling Chanel trying to start a dialogue. She even stalked her on social media by constantly sending friend requests and following the same people in her network and friends of Chanel.

Chanel never thought to share his Chad's new love interest's intentions because she simply thought he would be smarter than that. Besides, at the time it started Chad was still married to Audrey and the woman had children and was also married to someone else. Now she figured Chad actually was not smart enough, at least, not to recreate a situation where he'd get someone pregnant that he's not married to, but she was wrong. Instead for months she avoided any talk with people about babies. She knew the only way the woman could ensure she would be a part of Chad and Chris' life was to bring to life something that would connect them. So Chanel resorted to changing the channel on TV when the pregnancy test commercials aired. It hadn't worked. Chad was choosing someone else over Chris…again.

Now this woman was suggesting she and Chanel should become allies since they both have a child by the same man. The proposal didn't appeal to Chanel.

It took everything within Chanel to make the best of what was growing into a horrible situation. Many were surprised, but understood when she went through with the move. After all, the whole purpose of the transition was not about their relationship, but his and Chris'. So the goal was still the same.

Knowing she couldn't count on Chad for anything, not even the move he asked her to do, she enlisted the help of an old friend to make the journey with her.

She and Dawson Ayers, her high school crush, kept in contact even after he got married six years before. Now he was divorced and available as well.

"You know I think you and I taking a four-day road trip across the country could actually be fun," Dawson suggested over the phone. He lived in Atlanta, so it would be the first real time they'd spent together in a long time.

"I know, right?" Chanel agreed. "It's been so long since we've seen each other, it will be nice to catch up face-to-face. When can you fly in?"

"I can be there on the 29th," he responded eagerly.

"Okay, perfect. We can head out early and be in town early Sunday morning," she confirmed

"Sounds like a plan," he agreed.

What the two didn't plan for was endless hours of bickering. Dawson complained about everything Chanel did or didn't do. She toiled with trying to accommodate her traveling companion in order to maintain her sanity. Dawson stayed a few days with Chanel to help her get settled into her new place, but by the time he left, they were both at peace with being distant friends moving forward. The match made in heaven she daydreamed about constantly since the 9th grade was not the perfect match she hoped it would be afterall.

Even though she hated every waking minute of being in San Francisco, Chanel was closer to her family. She remained hopeful about Chad's pledge, but of course he was not getting off to a promising start.

The first two weeks, Chanel was understandably focused on finding work. This necessity didn't seem to matter much to Chad, though. He had flown out to DC a month ahead to pick up Chris, so he wouldn't have to endure the long car trip. It also allowed for the father and son to spend Father's Day with each other, but

Chad brought Chris to Chanel the day after she arrived in town. Conveniently, Chad's family lived in town, but no one was available to watch Chris when Chanel landed job interviews. Chanel was left to work it out on her own, just like old times.

After finding work, she could see the motivation for relocating was getting further and further away. She called Chad one day to discuss visitation arrangements for Chris. They had been in San Francisco a month and Chad only picked up Chris once for a visit, and a regular schedule needed to be put in place if this was really going to work. She left a note for Chad in Chris' overnight bag. When he didn't respond after a week, she called him instead.

"I'm open to whatever suggestions or preferences you have about seeing Chris, just let me know," she offered.

"Well, I don't have an opinion one way or the other. You decide," Chad responded arrogantly as usual.

So, she decided. Chad would see Chris every first and third weekend, starting Friday after school until Monday morning, and one day during the week, as long as Chad let her know one day before and Chris completed his homework. It seemed fair and reasonable to Chanel. It was fair and reasonable to Chad too, for about a month. Then, he started canceling or not showing up at all.

"I won't be able to make it tomorrow. How about next week?" he would say.
Such was also the case for any activity or program he was invited to at Chris' school. The once seemingly-supportive father that was slighted when it came to being a part of Chris' young life found it difficult to make an appearance to cheer on Chris at his piano recitals, class productions and baseball games.

"Why did I bring my child here?" Chanel asked herself.

She could have sucked things up if Chris was benefiting, but clearly, he wasn't. She saw the disappointment on his face every time his father didn't come to see him. When he did pick up Chris, he took him to his grandparents' house and left him there for the weekend.

The greatest disappointment was with Chad's younger sister Teresa. She and Chanel had always shared a decent relationship. There was a time Chanel could count on getting a weekly phone call from her or their mother, just to check in when they were back in DC. Sometimes she would even send little Chris a greeting card just to say she missed him or was thinking about him. She was a sweet auntie until they moved back to California.

Chad and Chanel met in the CVS parking lot when he was scheduled to spend the weekend with Chris. It was a neutral location for the two of them. Shortly after one of their meetings, his sister called Chanel upset.

"Where do you get off telling Chris to bring his clothes back home with him?" She snapped. "You didn't send a change of clothes for him in the first place!"

"What the hell are you talking about?" Chanel retorted. She couldn't believe she had taken such an accusatory tone with her. "Chris said you told him to bring his clothes home, but you didn't send anything with him."

"First of all, you need to change your tone," Chanel interjected. "Second, I would never send my son to stay overnight with anyone and not make sure he has a change of clothes."

"Well, you didn't send him anything for him tonight," the woman charged.

"I didn't send him anything this time because he has clothes there that weren't returned to me after his last visit." Chanel was hot. "If you check with his grandmother you would know he also has a dresser drawer full of clothes, including underwear, in her guest room." Before Chanel could finish her last thought, the once-sweet auntie hung up the phone.

"That b--," Chanel stopped herself. "What is her problem?"

The conversation bothered Chanel so much she called Teresa the next morning. This is something she wouldn't normally have done, but their relationship had come to mean a lot to her. In the past, Chris' aunt had shown more concern and interest in his life than her own sisters or even Chad. Teresa didn't pick up, and she never returned Chanel's message.

When Christmas came that year, and Chad didn't ask for Chris to spend the holidays with him, Chanel decided she was definitely going back to Washington, DC. Until then, Chanel would have to find other ways to make the most of her time while there, and she did.

Alana's job had transferred her to San Francisco, too, a few years earlier. Carmen lived there too. It was nice having trusted friends in town she could hang out with, but Alana was preoccupied. She was newly engaged and planning a huge wedding along with her parents who lived in town, too. They and their children became Chanel's local family. Alana's younger brother, Franklin, acquired an interest in Chanel soon after, but she always had an excuse for why they couldn't go out each time he asked. One day she finally agreed.

"Why are you always giving me such a hard time?" he asked.

Smiling Chanel replied, "I do not give you a hard time. I just know we are wrong for each other."

"Well, I happen to believe we are perfect for each other," he rebutted.

"Really?"

"Really, I do!" he said convincingly.

Franklin was a sophomore in college and Chanel was not! But it didn't seem to matter; the two were inseparable for months. It was easy for Chanel to block off any chance of catching feelings for the much younger man, but Franklin was all in. Chanel had never met anyone who wanted to make her happy all the time, not even Langston. At every given opportunity, Chanel reminded Franklin of her plans to move back across the country. He was having no parts of it.

"I want you to stay here… with me," he said

Hesitating, Chanel spoke, "You know I can't do that. I'm not happy here."

"I thought I made you happy?" Franklin questioned.

"You do, but I know it's only temporary. You're still in school and you have so much to experience and accomplish," she explained.

"I can finish school anywhere," he argued. "I've even thought about finishing school in DC."

"Oh, boy," Chanel thought to herself. "I hope he's not serious."

If he didn't finish school, Franklin's family would blame her for his decision. Plus, bringing a guy to live with her and Christopher was not the image of a family she hoped her son would have someday. Franklin needed to be discouraged from that notion.

When she wasn't tackling problems on the domestic front, professional woes could always be counted upon to occupy Chanel's time.

Since Chanel had been working as a paralegal for years in DC, it was only natural she'd continue on that path in the Bay Area. Besides, the pay in that field was not too shabby. Working could be her escape from what was happening in her personal life. The only problem was somehow Chanel had a special talent for selecting the most ridiculous companies and equally ridiculous managers to work for.

Larson & Haines was no different from those in the past. It was a big shot, downtown firm specializing in defending medical malpractice and wrongful death claims. Not her forte, but it would have to do. Chanel was hired to support two of the most unreasonable attorneys she'd worked with to date. Alice Larson was one she was sure had been sent by Satan directly to siphon off every ounce of peace and positivity in the atmosphere. As controlling as her old boss Brad was, he was never evil.

Somehow, this woman got it in her mind that it was necessary that every email she received in her inbox needed to be printed before it could be read. She felt so strongly about it that she gave Chanel access to her inbox in order to print her emails daily. Most days, the emails in Alice's inbox numbered in the hundreds. What this woman needed was a personal assistant, not a paralegal. Chanel would take every opportunity to educate Alice on her responsibilities as paralegal, which caused a series of disagreements between the two.

"Alice, I really don't have time to print emails today. I'm supposed to be preparing interview questions for a medical expert's testimony for Kelly's trial," Chanel would try to excuse herself. Kelly Haines was the other attorney Chanel supported.

Alice eyed Chanel from over the top of her eyeglasses before taking them off and placing them on her desk and asking, "Really? When is Kelly's trial starting?"

"The trial begins a week from today," Chanel explained.

"So, you have time then," Alice sarcastically suggested.

"No, actually I don't. I spend way too much time on menial administrative tasks like printing and stapling emails together, when those hours should be expended on more meaningful responsibilities like trial prep." The words had spilled out before Chanel realized how undone Alice had become.

"If I ask you to do something to help me, you are required to do it." By now Alice was standing and speaking to her from behind her desk with her arms folded.

"Well, I have a responsibility to set priorities, and in my opinion, preparing these questions takes priority over printing emails. So please talk it over with Kelly if you feel otherwise," She said arguing her point.

Chanel made a 90-degree turn out of Alice's office doorway and headed towards her desk. She could feel a flurry of cold air soar over her shoulder as hurricane Alice stormed past her in route to her colleague's office.

"The two of them will have to work it out," she said to herself. "But I will not spend an entire day printing emails!"

Kelly and Alice were both just starting their second careers and had everything to prove. Kelly had been a flight attendant before entering law school, and Alice a nurse. Of all the attorneys in the firm, these two kept the latest hours and spent more weekends in the office than the cleaning service. Chanel had really picked winners this time. There was an office policy which allowed every employee a free Friday off every month, in which accrued personal leave time and didn't have to be used. Of course, Chanel's free Friday was always the day Alice or Kelly or Alice and Kelly wanted her to come in to work. One Friday in particular was the day before Chris' birthday. The entire team was preparing for a big case the following week and all hands were on deck.
"You guys should also plan to be here tomorrow and Sunday to finish up what we don't accomplish today," Alice said as she addressed the support team.

"Has everyone met Rosalyn?" Kelly asked. "She was brought in yesterday from the temp agency and she will be here to help fill in the gaps for a while."

"Hi everybody," Rosalyn addressed the room. Rosalyn was very petite, with big brown eyes and a cute, round face. She was a few years older than Chanel, but her small stature made her appear much younger.

As everyone else from the team chimed in to make the new girl feel welcomed, Chanel pulled Kelly aside and said, "I told you I have a birthday party planned for my son tomorrow."

"Well, we need as many people this weekend as we can get." Kelly responded back.

"I can come on Sunday, but not tomorrow," Chanel agreed.

"Plan to come Sunday, but let's just see how the rest of today goes," Kelly rolled her beady green eyes and walked away. Alice and Kelly both left early that day, and even though it was supposed to be Chanel's Friday off, she and Rosalyn stayed late packaging materials that were to be overnighted to co-counsel in Las Vegas.

The next day was Saturday, Chris' party day. Chanel hosted it as planned without giving a thought to the office. On Sunday, she went in as promised, but no one was there. Within five minutes of arriving, Alice called her on her desk phone.

"What are you doing there?" she asked with annoyance in her voice already.

"I came in to work as I said I would," Chanel reminded her.
"Well, we finished everything yesterday when you weren't there. So, there's no need for you to be there now." Alice was pissed.

"Ok. See you tomorrow then." Chanel hung up the phone, checked her emails and left.

The "Laverne and Shirley duo" were bitter over the situation for the next couple of weeks. They called Chanel in for a meeting about their disappointment with her for not being there for the team. Chanel let it all roll off her back because she had already decided her time there was coming to an end. She and Chris would be back in DC before she knew it. That assurance didn't make coming in to the office any easier, though. One morning, Chanel called in to Kelly and lied about not being able to come in to work. She told her her house key had broken off into the dead bolt and she needed to wait for apartment maintenance to come by to repair it.

"There's no way I can leave my house unlocked," Chanel explained to Kelly over the phone.

"Sure, I understand," Kelly replied. "Guess we'll see you when you get here."

Chanel wasn't really sure whether her story was convincing or not, but she really didn't care. Her welcome at Larson and Haines was wearing thin, and fast.

She and Rosalyn, the temp, were becoming friends quickly. Chanel invited her to lunch one day, and they discovered they had a lot in common.

"So, you have a son, right?" Rosalyn inquired.
"Yeah, his name is Christopher." Chanel responded.

"Shut up!" Rosalyn joked. "Really? My son's named Kristopher too, but I spell it with a 'K'."

"Ahh, that's cool. How old is he?" Chanel inquired.

"He's nine, but he'll turn 10 next month," she answered.

"Girl, get out of here - my Chris is nine too!" They both laughed. "How funny is that?" Chanel reasoned.

"I know, right?" Rosalyn smiled.

The women were both single moms. Ironically, Rosalyn was also born in Texas, just like Chanel, and neither of them thought too highly of the fathers of their children. It felt good to have a new friend she could relate too. Chanel rarely met someone who truly understood her position and why her situation with Chad caused her so much grief.

In the spring, things really began to take a turn with Chad, and not for the better. Somehow, Chanel convinced him to take Chris for a few days while she went out of town for a work meeting, only she didn't really have a work trip at all. She flew to DC to find an apartment in preparation for their return. When he found out work wasn't the reason for the trip, he began to speculate her trip had to do with another man, and he confronted her the night she came back into town. He had an issue as if he was her man still.

"I know you didn't have to go to any work meeting," he said that night. "But it's cool."

"Don't you even begin to think you know anything about me or my job, Chad." Chanel spoke calmly, realizing Chris may have given up her plans to move back to the east coast to his father.

"Yea, I know all about your weekend rendezvous with Alana's brother," Chad continued.

Chanel, somewhat tickled, replied, "What I do and whomever I do it with is no business of yours. I would appreciate it if you stayed out of mine."

"I will make myself a part of your business as long as it has an impact on my son," he said.

Laughing out loud, Chanel replied, "Your son? Ha! Now you want to have some say so? Man, please go take a seat somewhere."

"Yes, my son! He's my son too, you know!" Chad raised his voice, drawing attention from the onlookers in the parking lot.

"Well, it's a little late for you to start acting like it now," Chanel angrily responded.

"Maybe you should remember he's your son all of the time, and not only when it's convenient for you, or just when you want to show him off.," she said letting out some long-held frustrations.

"Christopher, let's go." She yelled and motioned for the child who was still strapped into the back seat of his father's SUV.

Chad was verbally abusive in his text messages to Chanel after that. He started sending coded text messages to threaten her when she didn't do what he wanted her to. The thought sounded crazy; moving across the country AGAIN. She had to be a fool.

"No, wait. It was foolish to move back to San Francisco in the first place," she reminded herself.

Chad was never going to change, and now he was becoming down right mean. Chanel cried night after night worried about who Chad spent more time with, and wondering if perhaps he loved his other child more than Christopher. In her mind, it was unfair of him to give the impression to everyone that he was super dad with one kid but fail miserably with his first child. Who could Chad fool? He was incapable of being a good father to anyone. Chanel had essentially delivered their son to his door step and he was still rejecting him. She gave him everything he said he needed to be there for Christopher, but she never got any thanks for her sacrifice - only criticism and an extreme lack of cooperation. All of that and he still didn't deliver in his promise.

She had to go back. Her son deserved better, and Chanel would see to it that he got it.

"So, you're really going through with it?" Rosalyn asked.

"Yes, ma'am. I'm more sure about it now that I was before," Chanel explained.

"Why? What do you mean?" Rosalyn was curious.
"Last Saturday he showed up late to Christopher's baseball game with an announcement. He came to let me know he has a new job, but he has to relocate to Los Angeles."

"LA? Are you serious? That is a shame," her friend agreed.

Chad had quit his job in San Francisco two months after the judge ordered an increase of $500 in his child support. He was so angry about the verdict he chose to be unemployed rather than pay that amount to Chanel. It didn't matter that for most of Chris' life, the first order Chad received when they were back in college was the only order of record, and Chad wasn't even honoring that. Now, he wanted to move to Los Angeles where his new baby was, abandoning Christopher who just moved across the country to be close to him. Chanel always suspected the new order also infuriated his sister, which explained her extreme change in attitude towards her and Chris.

Chanel kept her secret for months. For her own sanity, she kept the information from Chad until the last possible moment. Otherwise, she would spend the remaining time defending her decision in persistent arguments with him and his family about her choice. By withholding the information, she had to endure the drama just a few weeks.

"Girl, before I knew it, I had blurted out that he could keep his excuses because Chris wouldn't need them anymore in DC."

"So you finally told him" Rosalyn inserted. " He must have hit the roof!"

"I really don't know if he's angry, Rosalyn," she answered. "I sent it over a text. I haven't heard from him yet, but at least now when Chris has a school event, his father living in another state will be an honest excuse for him not to show up."

They were literally days away when she told Chad's family. She saw that the news saddened his mother, but for Chanel, it was too little, too late. Though she personally grew to like Chad's mom, even she couldn't convince her to stay. Exactly one year to the day she moved there, Chanel found herself trudging back east hopeful, but once more, unsure of their future.

I gave him a chance, she thought as she stared out of the airplane window. I know I have done everything I can do to salvage his relationship with his child. Now it's up to him.

She accepted, for the first time, that some things just have to die. And she had to let it go in order to have something new.

One of the main differences between her and Chad was that she wasn't afraid to leave people or relationships behind if it meant improving things for her child. Chanel only wanted Chad to be as passionate about their son's life as she was. It was clear he hated her for that. He never supported or appreciated her reasons for doing so. Every voicemail he left on her cell phone in the days that followed was vulgar and insulting. Chanel had shared with him major disappointments in her relationship with her own father. He was aware of her pain and began using it against her as a weapon. Chanel knew that Chad had always been irresponsible and even inconsiderate in all the years she had known him, but now he had become down right hateful. He was so obsessed with picking fights with her, she restricted their communication to email only. Even then he was more concerned with hurting her than their son.

She'd made a deposit and signed a lease on that weekend work trip to DC. So at least this time, Chanel and Chris had a place of their own to go home to. Her only goal now was saving as much money as she could before starting law school.

Chanel didn't find work right away. In fact, it was two months before she found full time work. When she did, she couldn't have anticipated how this new gig would change her life yet again.

CHAPTER THIRTEEN

S tarting a new job is always difficult. It's like the first day of school, but for grown-ups. You don't have any friends, except the teacher, or, in the case of a new job, your new supervisor. All you can do is hope to get through the day without doing or saying anything stupid. Chanel pulled it off, and this time, she was sure things would be different. She had a lot of hope for this risk assessment firm and she was looking forward to her future there. It was time for a do-over in a lot of her life. Chanel had just spent the last year in a situation she hated. So, this was a very welcomed changed.

Everything Chanel had been through and all she'd experienced had led her to this very moment. It was a defining moment, and the time came for her to recover all that she'd lost.

This time, I'm going to get it right, she thought as she grabbed her purse to leave.

"So, how was your first day?" someone asked.

Chanel turned to see the source of the baritone voice she heard from behind. Not expecting a sound so rich to come from the mouth of a man like this, she smiled back and said, "It went well. Thanks."

She turned back around to exit the front door. As she crossed the empty parking lot and activated the remote to unlock her car, she was again delighted by the sound. This time he said, "Have a good night."

She quickly replied, "You too."

"I have a new focus and goals," Chanel repeated as she drove home that night.

As the first day turned into the first week, and the first week into the first month, Chanel was surprised daily by the kindness of the coworker with the sexy voice. The guy from the parking lot didn't exactly fit her definition of ideal, which is why she was a bit uncomfortable when she began to notice sexual chemistry between the two of them. It was subtle at first—as it always is. He worked as an attorney there and had been with the company several years.

"Just give me a call if you need anything else," he'd say as he left her office for the third time that morning.

Chanel found herself making up excuses to have him stop by, and he did the same. Then, there were the cute gazes into each other's eyes, the extra special visits to each other's offices just to say hello. She always left room for the possibility of falling for someone at work, but Chanel never believed it would actually happen. She always hoped to work with someone she was attracted to, and Lance was perfect for her. Tall, sexy, smart and more than that, he considered her more than any other man had ever done.
Chanel knew she was feeling him a little too much when she started talking about him with her best friend, Alana.

"I could tell him anything and he wouldn't judge me. He understands me when so many others in my past couldn't or wouldn't," she said.

"Oh, my God. You really like him, don't you?" Alana teased.

"Are you kidding me? That's my boo!" She said. Of course, Lance grew to like his nickname.

The beautiful thing was that they discovered their feelings for each other were mutual, which pleased them both. The problem was that Lance was separated, but not yet divorced. The fact that he was also Asian only served to complicate the situation further, but he seemed to become the man of her dreams and everything she'd been praying for.

"What about his family? How would they respond to him replacing his white wife with a black girlfriend?" she asked herself.

"The fact that I'm a black single mother doesn't help my cause either." It would never work. Chanel tried hard to talk herself out of her feelings for this new guy and it worked. They managed to keep everything pretty cool for a while. She went out with someone else and Lance couldn't take it. Chanel made the mistake of telling him about her date plans beforehand, and he sent her text messages the entire time hoping to distract her and keep him in mind the entire time.

"I hope you enjoy yourself today," he wrote at first.

When she didn't reply, he wrote, "But not too much."

Later on, when she got home, Lance called. He said he just wanted to make sure she made it in safely. Chanel thought his jealousy was very cute. No other guy seemed to care that much. Then one day while involved in one of their tit-for-tat middle school arguments over the office fax machine, it happened–the "Look."

Lance stood there staring intensely for those five seconds, and he had to physically shake his head to release his gaze that was transfixed into her brown eyes.

I'm in love with this man, Chanel thought. Oh, God that's not what I wanted, but it's happening.

Now, she looked forward to going into work every day more than before. She had to see him and wanted him to see her too. Lance always had something flattering to say about what Chanel was wearing or how she styled her hair. They went to lunch together every day, desperately trying to keep their adoration of each other a secret. Ironically their secret was discovered during an office luncheon. Both had taken their food back to Lance's office to eat together in private. In their usual playful way, the couple took opposing views on a random topic and Chanel jabbed him in his shoulder.

"Oh, so you're abusing me now?" he joked.

"That was nothing," she insisted. "I could have socked you in your jaw."

"I would like to see that," he urged.

"And what would you do about it? Not a thing!" she teased. As she attempted to walk away, he grabbed her by the waist pulling her into his lap. He'd been sitting behind his desk. He asked, "Now what? You can't say a word now, can you?"

Lance leaned in for a kiss and Chanel didn't stop him. Before she knew it, the two were in a lip lock that neither of them had anticipated. Seconds into it, a coworker passed by the door, and seeing the two in such a position, the woman let out a gasp. Chanel sprang from his lap before the eye witness could walk away, horrified that someone had seen them.

"Why didn't you close the door Lance?" Chanel asked slapping his shoulder.

"How was I supposed to know this was going to happen?" he said.

"Oh, my God! Do you think she will tell?" Chanel asked worried.

"Diane? Nah, she won't tell," he tried to make Chanel relax, but it didn't work.

Pacing the floor now, Chanel scratched her head in a panic.

"It's fine Chanel. Don't worry about it," he tried again to comfort her.

"I know she's going to tell. I just know she will. Did you see the look on her face? There's no way she going to keep quiet about this. I wouldn't," she said assured.

Lance sat back in his chair, his hands across his face. "Look, we're all adults here. Who cares whether we kiss? Don't ruin it, Chanel. It was a nice moment and personally I'm glad it happened," he said with a smile.

Chanel blushed. "It was nice, huh?" she agreed.

Lance got up from his chair and walked towards her. He took hold of Chanel's hands and kissed her soft lips again, and then her forehead. "Like I said, don't worry about it." The two embraced. Chanel melted in his arms and thought, Sure I could lose my job, but this man is so wonderful.

Two weeks passed without so much as a hint of any office gossip. Maybe Lance was right, Chanel decided. I guess Diane hasn't told anyone.

Chanel was loving life. She finally had a job she could tolerate. All her legal experience had helped her transition into a new field, and she was enjoying her new gig as a Claims Analyst. Lance's divorce was now final and she was planning a trip to Atlanta for Thanksgiving with him. Rosalyn was flying down for her birthday weekend and suggested they meet up there.

"Girl, I can't wait to meet this mystery man of yours," Rosalyn said. "What's his name again?"

"His name is Lance and you're going to love him." Chanel assured her. She had conveniently left out the fact that he was not black. She didn't want anyone to have the chance to develop preconceived notions of the kind of person he was before they met him.

Chanel figured she would have Lance meet a few of her friends first before meeting family. Perhaps she would have a better indicator of how her family would react.
Things were finally looking up. That's why Chanel wasn't prepared for the devastating blow just around the corner.

The next morning, November 19th—Chanel always made special note of that day—it was Langston's 32nd birthday. It had been a while since they last spoke, but Chanel wanted to seek him out to send him a well wish for this year of his life. As she drove into work that morning, she remembered how she felt eight years ago when he called to tell her he was getting married to the mother of his second child, Alexis. Throughout all of the transitions and challenges she had faced in life, her love for Langston never wavered. The short-lived college sweethearts always picked up where they left off when they spoke to one another again.

After the e-mail she sent came back as undeliverable, Chanel entered a Google search for Langston Bryant.

It sure would be nice to hear his voice, she thought, as she vetted the phone numbers that appeared on Peoplesearch.org and peeked at a few other hits in her list of results. Her attention, however, was drawn to an article in the search results. Someone named Langston Bryant as one of two victims found murdered in a burnt vehicle off a California highway. Chanel opened the link to read more:

A judge has delayed a trial for a man accused of murdering a woman in an Ester apartment, stabbing a man in Fairbanks the same day and conspiring to kill three other people.
"Oh, my goodness!" Chanel gasped as she read in disbelief.

She continued to read. Jason Wallace was scheduled to go on trial in March for allegedly attempting to murder Corey Spears of Fairbanks. Wallace's trials could be the first chance for the public to learn the circumstances surrounding a bizarre chain of events that started with the murder of Langston S. Bryant, 25, of Fairbanks, Alaska.

"This can't be my Langston. God, no," she said in disbelief.

Chanel opened the next search result. It read similarly, the bodies of two young African-American males had been discovered by the highway patrol responding to a car fire off a Northern California highway in the early morning hours of April 9, 2002. One of the victims was presumed to be 25-year-old Langston S. Bryant of ...

Chanel couldn't read any further. She covered her mouth with her hands as she began to hyperventilate. A stream of tears soon followed. The only thing she could think to do was call Alana. When Alana picked up her phone, Chanel blurted out, "Langston is dead!"

"What?" Alana answered back.

Chanel responded hysterically, "I'm reading a page on the internet about a Langston Bryant being found dead in 2002."

"Chanel, wait a minute. Please calm down. Are you sure it's him?" Alana tried to reason. It was no use.

"The article says the victim was from Fairbanks, Alaska and he was 25 years old." Struggling to catch her breath, she continued. "Alana, how many black men named Langston from Fairbanks would have been 25 years old in 2002?"

"Chanel, you have to try to calm down. Just breathe." Alana advised. "Where are you right now?"

"I'm at work. I just got here a few minutes ago." Chanel tried hard to hold back the tears.

"Maybe you should leave for the day," her friend suggested. "Just let someone know that you just received some upsetting news and you have to go home. Where is Lance?"

"I don't know," Chanel replied. "I don't think he's in yet."

"Okay, well just contact your supervisor and let him know what's going on and go home. You shouldn't be there right now. Not like this. I will stay on the phone with you while you drive home."

Chanel was flabbergasted. "How could something like this happen, Alana?" she questioned. Tears were flooding her face and neck now. "I will call you later," she said, and hung up the phone.

She headed to her car feeling her heart breaking into pieces. Lance shouted to her as she began to drive away. Chanel didn't care. She was too upset. Almost instantaneously, she felt her cell phone vibrating in her coat pocket. It was Lance.

"Good morning beautiful, I just saw you leaving," he said. "You looked upset. Are you okay?"

"No. I'm not okay," Chanel sobbed. "I just found out my ex-boyfriend is dead."

"What?" Lance was genuinely stunned. "I'm so sorry, sweetheart," he consoled. "Where are you going right now?"
"I really can't be at work right now. I'm going home," she said.

"I can meet you at your house," Lance offered.
"No, it's fine. I need some time to myself," she declined.

"Are you sure?" he questioned. "I can be there in an hour."

"I'm sure. I- I just really need some time to think." Chanel insisted.

"Okay, if you're sure. I will call you back in a little while to check on you."

"Okay." Chanel ended the call and burst into tears again. There was no way this could be true. Maybe she misread something. In the back of her mind she really didn't believe it was a mistake.

When she got home, she grabbed some tissue from the bathroom and curled up on the sofa. Her head was pounding now from all the crying. Her mind was overwhelmed with memories of when she met her first true love. She could recount her first phone conversation with Langston verbatim. Chanel didn't understand how something so awful could happen to someone who was so sweet. She would probably never know what brought Langston's life to such a dreadful end, and that made her ache even more. She needed to get herself together; Christopher would be home from school before she knew it, and he couldn't see her this way.

After sobbing for some time, Chanel didn't even realize she had dozed off.

She woke up later completely numb on her right side. She tried to sit up, but her head was as heavy as a ton of bricks.
"Am I paralyzed?" she asked out loud, not knowing whether she was alone in the room or not.

"Oh, my Lord," a familiar voice billowed back to her. "Someone get the doctor. She's awake. She's awake!" the voice shouted.

It sounded like the voice was speaking from under water to Chanel.

"No baby, you're not paralyzed." It was Nannie. Chanel could feel her grandmother's warm, soft hands petting her face.

Nannie? How did she get here? she thought to herself.

"Where is my baby?" Chanel asked concerned. "Where is Christopher?" She tried to focus her eyes, but her vision was blurred. Adding to the confusion was the sound of her own voice she spoke with. It was high pitched, like that of a child.

Chanel struggled to understand what was happening.

"Who is Christopher, sweetheart?" Nannie asked, assuming her seven-year-old granddaughter must be hallucinating.

Just then the doctor arrived.

"Oh my, what do we have here?" The handsome doctor walked over to Chanel's bed. He retrieved his medical pen flashlight from his pocket and shined it into each of the youngster's eyes.

"What am I doing here?" Chanel was anxious for an explanation.

"Hello, sweetheart, can you tell me your name?" the doctor asked.

"My name is Chanel," she replied.

"Unbelievable," the doctor muttered under his breath. "Chanel, do you know where you are right now?" he asked.
She did not respond.

The doctor questioned her again, "Do you remember being hit by a car?"

"Yes. When I was a little girl," her speech was slurring now.

"Is she okay, Dr. Langston?" the grandmother questioned.

"Please try not to be too alarmed just yet, ma'am." he said. "She's just regaining consciousness. This confusion may only be temporary."

"This is great news," he continued. "But we're going to need to take her down to neurology for some cognitive testing." The day Chanel was hit by the car, she suffered a serious head injury. It was enough to knock her unconscious. The tall, handsome doctor with the beautiful, white teeth had been her primary physician since the accident. He was in charge of monitoring her progress daily until she was stabilized.

"Nurse, please contact her parents immediately and find Dr. Bradley," the doctor ordered.

"Yes, doctor." the nurse replied.

Nannie bolted for the room telephone in one direction and the nurse headed for the nurse's station in the other.
Chanel tried to sit up again, but she was tied down. The doctors had ordered that for her safety. They feared she might wake up when she wasn't being monitored, curiously wander off and possibly hurt herself in the process.

Before she knew it, Nannie had placed the cold telephone against her ear.

"Nel, is that really you?" the familiar voice asked through the receiver.

"Say hello, baby," her grandmother urged. "It's your mama."

"Mama," Chanel tried to mumble back.

"Chanel! Chanel. Oh, my God. I can't believe it!" Kathy went on. "Oh, thank God you're okay!"

"Mama, what happened to me?"

"Oh, Chanel I've been praying I would hear your voice again. I'm going to call your daddy and we will be there real soon to see you, okay?"

"Yes, mama," Chanel thought. The room was spinning now. A duo of neurologists, Dr. Bradley and Dr. Brown, along with several other hospital staff soon flooded the room poking, prodding, and checking her everywhere.

They tried to keep the child awake by calling her name and patting her hand. The doctors were concerned if she fell asleep so soon she would slip back into the coma. Chanel relented and the room went black.
She woke up again about 30 minutes later, trembling to the sound of laughter and the slow, dull hum of machines.

The staff members from the pediatrics and radiology departments of Bridgewood Memorial Hospital were all there. Chanel had been in a coma for the past 30 days. Nannie, Joe, and Aunt Juanita had taken alternating shifts at the hospital to make sure someone was there in case she woke up. Kathy was still in recovery because of the car wreck last summer and could never stay long to watch over her daughter.

"Don't worry, little one. I'm right here. I'm not leaving you." The voice sounded familiar. Chanel peered through the cracks in her eyes again, trying to make out the face of the young woman standing over her looking down from a pair of beautiful green eyes as big as saucers.

"Hi there," the woman spoke again. "I've been waiting to talk to you, Chanel. My name is Alana and I am a nurse."

Chanel replied back, "A-Alana?"

"Yes, Alana. Can you spell Alana?" she asked.

The seven-year-old had always been very sharp in school. She tried to sound it out, "A-l …", but she stopped short.

"It's okay, sweetie," the nurse added. "That was really good. I wanted to come down with you to make sure you're okay. You don't have to be afraid of anything because I will be right here.

"Hello Chanel," another voice spoke up from behind. "My name is Dawson. I'm going to be doing a special test on your brain today, okay? It's called an MRI and I have to put you inside this big machine."

Chanel looked at the man puzzled.

"It's not going to hurt you, but you have to lie very still and not move," he said.

The little girl wondered, Do I know this man?

By the time the test was complete, Joe and Kathy had made it to the hospital and were waiting in her room. Kathy was using a walker now, no longer needing a wheel chair. She hobbled to

Chanel's bedside.

"Nel, can you hear me?" Kathy asked.

Even though she recognized her mother's face, Chanel couldn't respond.

Kathy addressed the doctor. "Can she hear me, Dr. Brown?"

"Yes, I'm sure she can," he replied. "It's also very possible she has been able to hear and comprehend everything that's been going on around her this past month as well."

The family of the little girl sharing a hospital room with Chanel couldn't help but share in the excitement. Their daughter, Tori had been admitted a couple weeks after Chanel for a bone marrow transplant. Tori's mother offered a celebratory hug for Kathy and Joe.

"I'm so happy for you," she said.
"We've been praying for a miracle and we got one. I still can hardly believe it." Joe stood silent next to Kathy and began to cry.

Chanel had dozed off again. She was exhausted by all the excitement. She was unaware of all the well-wishers and medical professionals stopping in to take notes and observe. Later, the nurse working the evening shift named Charlotte came in to relieve Alana. Most of the traffic of visitors had died down and things were quiet.

"This is just the kind of news I needed," Charlotte began. She and Alana sat chatting at the nurse's station. "Ever since my brother Brian passed away, I've been desperate to find something to be happy about."

Alana embraced her friend. "I know things have been hard for you," she sympathized. "And I don't know how this family would have coped if Chanel didn't pull through."

"No one should have to suffer through that, but knowing she made it has really lifted my spirits." Charlotte took a deep breath in and exhaled.

"Well, I have to get out of here," Alana said. "I have to make that long drive out to Fresno to pick up Christopher tonight."

Charlotte questioned. "You mean Chad won't bring him back home? What else does he have to do? He quit his job."

The two women could go on for hours discussing Alana's domestic situation. They had been friends since high school, and like most coworkers, they shared their life experiences with one another on a daily basis. Alana was a single parent, with constant conflicts with her son's father. Charlotte was working through the death of her twin brother and the tumultuous relationship she had with her dad. The two best friends were never at a loss for topics to discuss, and sleeping Chanel bared witness to most of their conversations.

The women liked to stay current on the office scandals, too. One of the biggest ones involved two x-ray technicians named Kelly and Alice. A fist fight broke out once between the two in the breakroom. Alice slapped Kelly after finding out Kelly had been sleeping with her little sister Audrey's husband. It was by far the most violent hospital scandal at Bridgewood.

"Okay, Charlotte," Alana said as she packed up her things. "Enough of my drama with Chad for tonight. We will catch up on late breaking news tomorrow. Have a good night."

"You too, and drive safely," Charlotte cautioned.

Alana had been driving the same beat up Mustang for ten years, since high school.

Over the next few days, young Chanel's recovery was slow but steady. Even with all of the testing their daughter was subjected to, her family became more and more hopeful every day. Her doctors worked non-stop, making notes of even the most miniscule of improvements.

Alana came in routinely every morning to give the youngster a sponge bath. When she did, she would turn on the television in Chanel's room so that she could watch her favorite daytime drama, And the Time Came, while she worked.

One morning when Alana walked into her room, Chanel was already sitting up in bed wide awake.

"Good Morning, Sunshine!" Alana greeted her warmly. "Don't you look pretty today?"

The little girl had a big, bright smile on her face and big yellow bows in her hair to go along with it. Aunt Juanita had spent the night and woke early to comb her niece's hair.

Chanel smiled a gentle smile, not recognizing Alana's face at first, but certainly remembering her voice.

"You can take a break now, if you need one," Alana directed Juanita. "I know you're exhausted."

Stretching as she rose from the uncomfortable mini sofa, Juanita agreed. "You're right about that. I should take a shower and freshen up." She gathered her things and headed for the bathroom.

Chanel continued to follow the nurse around the room with her eyes when all of a sudden, the child blurted out, "Where is Christopher?"

Alana was stunned.

"Christopher?" she questioned. "How do you know Christopher?"

"I know Christopher. You take care of him too," Chanel replied.

Alana's eyes began to swell with tears. She sat next to Chanel on the bed and began to rub her small hands.

"Who else do you know, sweetheart?"
Instantaneously, Chanel's attention was drawn to the music on television. Alana had flipped on the box when she came in that morning as usual. The child stared at the set in almost a trance.

"Do you know this show?" Alana asked.

Chanel didn't respond.

Alana pointed to the screen, asking the child to name the characters as they appeared scene after scene and began to speak. Chanel named them all, one by one. First, Rosalyn and Raymond, then Eddie and Emmanuel, Keith. She even knew Kyle, the show's heartthrob.

"This is unbelievable!" the doctor remarked.

The nurse briefed Dr. Langston on what she'd witnessed. "She even knew I have a son named Christopher. How do you explain that?" Alana challenged.

"It can only mean one thing," the doctor replied.

Alana looked more intrigued.

"What Dr. Bradley suspected was right. Chanel was able to hear everything going on around her the last 30 days. If not everything, certainly a lot of it."

Later, the doctors conferred. "She's been aware the whole time. The coma wasn't caused by the accident itself. It was secondary in the brain's efforts to achieve healing for the rest of the body."

"I don't think this little lady has suffered from any brain injury at all. We have to bring her family in to let them know the amazing news," the doctor explained with excitement.

"That explains it." Kathy exclaimed. She, Joe, and most of the family met with the team of medical staff to be updated on their findings.
"That explains how it is that she knew the name of the pastor from the radio, Pastor Fred Clark. On the days I came to visit her, I always listened to the gospel radio station in her room. Pastor Clark's show airs every day at noon. She had to be listening too."

"That is exactly why we are confident that your daughter has not sustained any brain injury," stated Dr. Brown. "This is also consistent with the scans we've recently taken as well as all the brain activity we captured while she was sleeping."

"Wait a minute. What are you saying doctor?" Joe asked.

"We're saying Chanel is ready to go home, Mr. Hamilton," Dr. Bradley advised with a smile. "We will, of course, continue to monitor her progress through weekly rehabilitation and follow up visits over the next six-to-eight weeks, but she is free to go home today.

"What? Really?" Kathy wondered out loud. "Is it safe?"

"Mrs. Hamilton," Dr. Brown chimed in, "It's more than safe, it's highly encouraged. Your daughter is very is young and strong. The sooner she's back into her home life, the sooner we all will see a full recovery. Her progression over the past two weeks since she awoke has been remarkable. Thanks to the physical therapy she received in bed while still sleeping, her body was able to retain a great percentage of muscle memory. She will be weaker than normal at first, but she will only improve rapidly at this point. That's the beauty of a young developing mind."

"What about school?" Kathy questioned. "Is she ready for school?"

"Our rehab therapist will work out a plan with Chanel's school curriculum. Don't worry. We will start slow, likely just one-half day next week and then build up to a week of half days. We'll let her progress and set her own pace," the doctor explained.

Joe gave Chanel the news.

She was understandably scared at first. Not really sure what to think. With all the changes over the past week, the child never really had a chance to even process what had caused her to be in the hospital anyway, or why her mind was being flooded with memories and images of the folks she met in her dreams. What was real, what was imagined?

"We're taking you home today, Nel." Joe explained.

"Home to Bakersfield?" Chanel wondered.

Joe, realizing the process was going to be a journey, kissed his little girl on the forehead and said, "No, sweetheart. Remember, we live in Jacksonville?"

Chanel remembered, but thought it was the home of her past.

Alana came by the next day to send off the family. "I want you to keep in contact with me, little one, okay?" she ask sincerely. Chanel nodded in agreement.

The drive home was painful, but not physically. That was the easy part. All the cuts and bruises had healed and the swelling had gone away. All that remained was a slight limp from a sprained hip. It had been nearly two months since Chanel was hit, but it felt like 20 years. Her entire life had been lived out in her dreams.

But was it really her life? It became clear, day-by-day, that what had been real was actually the lives of her caregivers. In her dreams, the child had gained more wisdom than most adults will acquire in a lifetime. She experienced love, heartbreak, joy and sorrow, rejection, humiliation, honesty, and commitment. In some ways, her pathways were now paved, but chartered in a direction.